The

TEAPOTS
ARE OUT
and other
ECCENTRIC
TALES *from*
IRELAND

The

TEAPOTS
ARE OUT
and other

ECCENTRIC
TALES *from*
IRELAND

John B. Keane

CARROLL & GRAF PUBLISHERS
NEW YORK

THE TEAPOTS ARE OUT
AND OTHER ECCENTRIC TALES FROM IRELAND

Carroll & Graf Publishers
An Imprint of Avalon Publishing Group Inc.
245 West 17th Street
New York, NY 10011

First Carroll & Graf edition 2004

Library of Congress Cataloging-in-Publication Data is available.

ISBN: 0-7867-1298-8

Printed in the United States of America
Distributed by Publishers Group West

CONTENTS

TO MY GRANDCHILDREN
WITH LOVE

1
FRED RIMBLE

Fred Rimble was born in Maggie Conlon's bedroom in Dirreenroe at three minutes past seven on the evening of 7 September 1979. The event was not marked by any unusual celestial manifestations nor was there the least furore in the more immediate circumjacence of Dirreenroe.

'Indeed,' said Maggie Conlon's son Jim at a later date, 'I would not have brought the poor creature into the world at all but for being driven to it by my mother's ear-ache.'

At seventy-five Maggie Conlon belied her age by several years. Her hair still retained most of its natural black. Her eyes were bright and clear. Her step was free of infirmity and while she would never admit to it the hearty appetite which she had enjoyed all her life still remained with her, completely unimpaired.

She should, therefore, have been fairly well pleased with the general state of her health and, of course, if you were also to take into account the fact that she was relatively well-to-do you should not be blamed for believing that her all-round lot was a happy one.

Alas the opposite was the case. Maggie Conlon was a hypochondriac. Local doctors could find nothing the matter with her but hope springs eternal so Maggie fared as far afield as her means would allow and consulted unsuccessfully with several noted specialists. She then resorted to quacks after the fashion of all true hypochondriacs and despite temporary cures of the most dramatic nature continued to provide local doctors and pharmacists with a solid source of income.

The mystery was that she managed to survive the vast and varied intake of potions and pills not to mention the liniments and lotions with which she harassed the countless aches and skin diseases to which her hypersensitive exterior seemed always to be prey. The most malignant aspect of this particular type of hypochondria was while it failed to hasten the demise of Maggie Conlon it had dispatched her two husbands to early graves.

Both had been hard-working men who needed rest and care after their day's labours. Neither, unfortunately, was forthcoming from Maggie. From dawn till dark both husbands were on call. Poultices were constantly in demand as were hot drinks, gargles and numerous other medicaments. These necessitated regular journeys upstairs and downstairs all through the night. Fine if Maggie was available in the morning to cook a sustaining breakfast and provide a nourishing lunch pack or if she was on her feet in the evening with a warm welcome and a warmer meal. Instead she was confined to bed and during those rare intervals when no pain troubled her she went around with her head and face muffled, with her body totally covered and smelling all the time of powerful prophylactics.

Whether or not she succeeded in warding off occupational diseases and wayward draughts was anybody's guess but one thing was certain. The germs of romance which might have blossomed in perfumed surrounds into rich and rewarding love were slowly but surely exterminated by the deadly disinfectants in which her garments abounded. The marriages had started out well enough. In the beginning there had been affection, a close relationship in both cases which might have been nurtured into something more rewarding if Maggie had shown the least desire to relinquish her unnatural pre-occupation with her health.

Jim Conlon was the sole outcome of the marriages presenting himself to the world shortly after the demise of his father, Maggie's second husband. At the time an unkind neighbour was heard to say that the poor man had precipitated his own death with the awful prospect that the issue might be female and that he would be faced with two Maggies instead of one. The truth was he died of fatigue. Maggie Conlon had worn him out just as she had worn out his predecessor. There are some men who thrive off selfish wives, who excel themselves as husbands in the face of such adversity. There are others who suffer in silence, waiting for death to rescue them. Maggie's pair were of this latter mould.

Her son Jim was a mild-mannered, easy-going fellow who asked little of the world. His job, a book-keeper in the local creamery, was undemanding. His wages were more than adequate. He lived with his mother. He might have married but progress in that direction was brought to an immediate halt as soon as any likely contender encountered Maggie.

One particular girl with whom he had made considerable headway spelled out her terms unequivocally after a visit to Maggie.

'I'm willing to marry you,' she told Jim, 'and I'm willing to devote the rest of my life to you but it will have to be in a town or city a long way from here.'

'I just can't walk out on her altogether,' he pleaded. 'After all she is my mother.'

'I'm not asking you to walk out on her,' the girl explained. 'You can visit her from time to time and she can visit us if she feels like it. You have your own life to live and I'm sure your mother will accept this when you explain it to her.'

'I never heard the like,' Maggie Conlon had retorted bitterly when Jim had laid his cards on the table. 'I mean it's not as if I were asking the pair of you to come and live with me under this roof and anyway where are you going to get another job if you leave Dirreenroe? Have you thought of that?'

'Oh I'll get another job all right,' Jim assured her. 'With my experience that should be no trouble.'

The following afternoon Maggie Conlon lay in a hospital bed as a result of an inexplicable collapse on her way from the butcher's earlier that morning. The doctors were mystified. Her heart was strong, her pulse steady, her blood pressure normal. She was released after a week with a clean bill of health after Jim had declared that he would never leave Dirreenroe.

Now at thirty-one he began, at last, to see the writing on the wall. The constant complaining had begun to take its toll. At work he wondered what new malaise would be awaiting him when he arrived home. It was not till he found himself on the threshold of mental disintegration that he brought Fred Rimble into the world. That morning before he left for work his mother had complained of a severe backache. Jim had called the family doctor but that worthy could find nothing wrong. When Jim arrived home for lunch his mother was still in bed. The ache in the back had removed itself and was now resident in the neck. When he finally finished work he was surprised to hear it had ended up in the left ear after a horrendous journey from its original starting place.

'I won't get a wink of sleep tonight,' she complained when he suggested she abandon the bed and share the stew which he had prepared for both of them. He pleaded in vain.

'I couldn't look at a bite,' she said which meant that she had eaten while he was at work. After he had washed and stowed the ware he returned to the bedroom. Her martyred face was barely visible through an opening in the red flannelette with which she had bound her head. The bed clothes were drawn tightly under her chin. Every so often a distraught moan punctuated her affected wheezing.

'No one has an ear like mine,' she whined.

'I don't know,' Jim spoke casually. 'A chap had his ear chopped off at the creamery today, his left ear.'

Maggie Conlon raised herself painfully on her elbows.

'Had his left ear chopped off?'

'His left ear,' Jim confirmed.

'Was he from Dirreenroe?' Maggie removed the red flannelette the better to catch the answer.

'From Dublin,' Jim confirmed.

'Oh the poor man.' Maggie was all concern. 'What hospital did they take him to?'

'No hospital,' Jim told her.

'But I don't understand. You say he had his ear chopped off.'

'Yes. He had his left ear chopped off.'

'And he didn't go to hospital?'

'As far as I know.'

Maggie sat upright in the bed. 'I'm afraid I don't understand.'

Jim rose from the side of the bed where he had seated himself. He sighed and went to the window. His gaze swept the evening sky before he spoke.

'He was demonstrating an electric potato peeler,' he explained slowly, 'and the next thing you know the damn thing

11

stopped. He bent down right where the potato goes in and off she starts without warning.'

'And the ear?'

'He put it in a bucket of ice and clapped a handkerchief over the wound and then hit for Dublin to have it sewn back on.'

'What did you say his name was?' Maggie Conlon asked.

'Fred Rimble,' Jim replied.

'I don't know any Rimbles,' Maggie said.

'How could you when he doesn't come from around here. I told you he came from Dublin.'

When he arrived home for lunch the following day he found his mother up and about. The pain in the ear had partially disappeared and for a change a hot meal awaited him.

'Any news of Fred Rimble?' Maggie asked.

Jim was taken unawares but he took advantage of a mouthful of mashed potatoes to hide his surprise. As he masticated needlessly his imagination worked overtime. Finally he spoke.

'He's lucky to be alive is Fred Rimble.'

'Did he get back to Dublin?'

'Not off his own bat. He fainted in the car from loss of blood and crashed into a telephone pole.'

'Oh my God!' Maggie Conlon cried. 'What happened then?'

'He was taken by ambulance to Dublin. Apparently the ice spilled from the bucket with the impact of the crash. The ear was thrown onto the roadway and could not be found. They fear a magpie may have made off with it or a grey crow or the likes.'

As his mother made the Sign of the Cross he hurriedly re-addressed himself to his meal. He realised her interest was thoroughly aroused. Bent over his plate he prepared himself for her next question.

'Is he married?'

'Yes.'

'Has he a family?'

'Eight. Four boys and four girls.'

'May God protect them,' Maggie Conlon whispered and she made the Sign of the Cross a second time.

Jim left for work earlier than usual. He needed time to think out a plan of campaign. He wondered how long he could continue with the deception. For the present he would do no more than release minor bulletins concerning the loss of the ear and the effects of same on Fred Rimble. Every weekend Jim Conlon spent most of his time in a neighbourhood tavern. He liked a few drinks and there was the added bonus of a reprieve from the pathological out-pourings of his mother. It was here he thought up the idea of providing Fred with a plastic ear.

'You're very thoughtful lately Jim boy,' Matt Weir the publican interrupted his conceptions.

'Friend of mine,' Jim explained, 'took a bad turn lately.'

'Sorry to hear that Jim boy.' Matt Weir patted him on the shoulder and moved off to comfort any other lone birds who might be on the premises.

A week after the accident Maggie took to the bed again. She blamed an old ankle injury which had been aggravated by a sudden change in the weather. Again Jim found himself fending for both of them. Maggie spent three full days in bed and might have spent three weeks had not Jim resorted to his friend Fred Rimble. When he returned for lunch on the third day he found her with the clothes tucked up to her chin. Her head was almost completely muffled by the red flannelette. The martyred look had returned to her face. The room reeked of recently-applied embrocation and every so often there were the old familiar sighs of untold suffering.

'This will be the death of me,' Maggie said.

Jim sat silently on the bed and carefully prepared his release.

'God alone knows what I go through,' Maggie groaned.

'Fred Rimble's wife left him.'

The announcement was made matter of factly. It took some time before Maggie was able to transfer from herself to this latest development.

'Was there another man?' she asked after a while.

'Afraid so,' Jim said.

'A neighbour I'll warrant.'

'Right first time,' Jim confirmed. 'His best friend to boot.'

Wisely Jim arose and left the room. Maggie's next question might prove too much for him. She was on her feet early the following morning. A fine breakfast awaited him when he came downstairs. While he dined Maggie spoke of the perfidy of neighbours. She roundly cursed the ruffian who stole Fred Rimble's wife.

Weeks were to pass before she took ill again, this time with nothing more than a crick in the neck. Maggie's cricks, however, were like no other. They might last for weeks or develop into far more sinister aches. Jim roused her by the simple expedient of telling her that Fred Rimble had broken both legs in another car crash. By the time the New Year was due Fred Rimble had, in addition to his earlier mishaps, broken his collar bone, both hands, numerous ribs and to crown his misfortune lost his second ear. It was the removal of the remaining auricle which provided Jim with the happiest Christmas he had spent since childhood. Maggie went around all through the festive period shaking her head and bemoaning the terrible loss. Her Christmas was, however, pain-free.

When he informed her about the second ear Maggie suggested that he contact Fred and invite him and the children to spend Christmas with them.

'No,' Jim had answered sagely. 'I know Fred. He's the sort of man who would want to spend Christmas at home.'

'But who's going to cook the Christmas dinner?'

'No problem there,' Jim informed her. 'The eldest girl is fifteen and then there's a woman nearby who looks in now and then.'

'What woman nearby?' Maggie asked suspiciously.

'Just a neighbour,' Jim replied.

Maggie searched his face to see if he was concealing anything. 'She wouldn't be by any chance the missus of the man who went off with Fred's wife?'

'No chance,' Jim assured her. 'Fred isn't that sort.'

'Of course not,' Maggie responded at once, 'that was not what I meant.'

Spring came round before she complained again. Normally she would have spent the greater part of January in bed and the remainder muffled up downstairs. Every week or ten days Jim would dole out what he privately termed a Rimble ration. Maggie awaited the titbits eagerly and gobbled up each and every one with relish. In January Jim was obliged to dispose by drowning of the eldest daughter whose name was Cornelia and of the youngest who answered to the name of Trixie. He had good reason for resorting to such extremes. His mother had taken suddenly to the bed one wet afternoon on the grounds that she had undergone a serious heart attack. Even the family doctor who knew her every gambit was perplexed.

'It is just possible,' he confided to Jim, 'that she may have suffered the mildest of coronaries.'

Jim sensed that a broken limb would not be sufficient this time nor indeed the loss of a hand or a leg. Her appetite had been whetted. She now needed stronger meat if a cure was to be effected. For this reason he felt obliged to dispose of Cornelia and Trixie. Maggie had jumped out of bed upon hearing the news, her heart miraculously cured.

'That's one funeral I'm not going to miss,' she announced. Try as he might Jim could not dissuade her. The following morning she rose early and purchased a daily paper. Painstakingly she went through the death notices.

'Rattigan, Remney, Reeves,' she intoned the names solemnly. 'Riley, Romney, Rutledge. There's no Rimble here.'

'I know Fred Rimble,' Jim said. 'Fred hates any sort of a show. The funeral would, of course, be private. That's why it's not in the papers.'

'We'll send him a telegram then,' Maggie insisted, 'and a letter of sympathy. I'll write it myself.'

'Of course,' Jim agreed. 'I'll send the telegram this very morning. You go ahead and write your letter and I'll post it for you during the lunch break.'

At his office in the creamery Jim burned the letter. A week later he typed a reply using a fictitious Dublin address. The letter proved the best tonic Maggie ever received. It kept her out of bed for several weeks. When its effects wore off he did away with the other children pair by pair, the first by food poisoning, the second by a car accident and the third by fire. Indeed Fred Rimble himself had been lucky to escape the conflagration with his life. The last proved to be a wise choice. Since the family home had been razed to the ground Fred was left without a permanent address.

The deaths of the Rimble children had a profound effect on Maggie. She took to attending early mass on a regular basis. Regardless of the weather she never once opted out. She enquired daily after Fred but news was scant. He had, it was reported, left the country and taken up work in Australia.

'Too many memories in the home place,' Maggie had observed when Jim informed her of Fred's departure. 'I imagine that if it were me I would do the very same thing,' she said wistfully.

Summer passed. Autumn russetted the leaves and the winds laid them out lovingly on the soft earth. Jim Conlon grew fat and content.

'There's a shine to you lately Jim boy,' Matt Weir told him one night.

Then winter came and inevitably Maggie Conlon took to the bed. In spite of assurances from her own doctor and from a specialist she became convinced that she was suffering from cancer of the throat. She submitted herself to X-rays and to countless other tests. The net result was that there was no evidence whatsoever to show that there was the least trace of the dread disease of which she complained. The weeks passed and when no decline set in she became even more insistent that cancer had taken hold of her windpipe. To prove it she fell back upon a comprehensive repertoire of wheezes, many of them spine-chilling, others weak and pathetic.

The contentment to which Jim Conlon had grown accustomed became a thing of the past. He lost weight. All the old tensions with some new ones in their wake returned to bedevil him. He tried every ruse to rouse his mother but all to no avail. She became so morbid in herself that she made him go for the parish priest every week. When the last rites were administered she would close her eyes as if resigning herself to death. In the end Jim was driven to his wit's end. One night he returned from the pub in what seemed to be a highly agitated state. In reality he was playing the last trump left in his hand.

'I've just had some dreadful news,' he informed his mother.

The lacklustre eyes showed no change nor did she adjust her position in the bed.

'Fred Rimble is dead,' Jim told her.

The news had the desired effect. At once she sat upright.

'How did it happen?' she asked after she had crossed herself and begged God's mercy on his soul.

'They say he died of a broken heart,' Jim informed her.

'A broken heart!' she exclaimed tearfully and wondered why she had never thought of this novel way out herself.

'That's what they said,' Jim spoke with appropriate sadness.

'Well it's all behind him now the poor man,' Maggie Conlon spoke resignedly. A few days later at Maggie's insistence they had a High Mass said for Fred Rimble in Dirreenroe parish church. It was an unpretentious affair with no more than the three priests, the parish clerk and themselves involved. As soon as they arrived home Maggie prepared lunch and when they had eaten she went at once to her bed vowing that she would never leave it.

'But what's wrong with you?' Jim asked in anguish. 'You were fine ten minutes ago. You put away a feed fit for a ploughman.'

'I know. I know,' she said weakly, 'but the bitter truth is that I think my heart is beginning to break.'

'This beats all,' Jim fumed.

'Now, now,' said Maggie. 'You mustn't let it upset you. It's not in the least like a coronary or angina. There's nothing like the pain. I'll just lie here now and wait for my time to come.'

She closed here eyes and a blissful look settled on her face.

In the tavern Jim sat on his own in a deserted corner. Midway through his third drink Matt Weir came from behind the counter and saluted him. When he didn't answer Matt asked if there was anything wrong.

'Look at me Matt,' Jim spoke despondently. 'Look at me and tell me what you see.'

'I see a friend and a neighbour,' Matt Weir answered.

'No Matt,' Jim countered. 'What you see is a man who killed the best friend he ever had.'

2
FAITH

The brothers Fly-Low lived in an ancient farmhouse astride a bare hillock which dominated their rushy fields. Tom Fly-Low was the oldest of the three. Next in age came Billy and lastly there was Jack.

Fly-Low, of course, was a sobriquet. The surname proper was Counihan. It was never used except by the parish priest once every five years when he read the Station lists.

In the year 1940 an Irish reconnaissance plane flew over the Fly-Low farm. At the time the brothers were in the meadow turning hay. As soon as the plane appeared they stopped work and lifting their hayforks aloft welcomed the unique intrusion. Acknowledging the salute the pilot dipped his wings.

'Fly low,' Jack Counihan called.

'Fly low,' shouted his brothers. 'Fly low, fly low,' they all called together. Alas the pilot was unable to hear them. In a few moments the plane had disappeared from view never again to be seen by the brothers Fly-Low. In neighbouring fields other haymakers heard the din. It was only a matter of time before the Counihans would become known as the Fly-Lows. It was no more than the custom of the countryside. It made for easy identification there being several other Counihan families in the nearby townlands.

Years later at the end of the Second World War there came one of the worst winters in living memory. When it wasn't awash with drenching rain the winds blew searingly and searchingly. There were times when it froze and times when it thawed, times too when it snowed till the hills turned white. In between there was sleet, that awful conglomeration which can never make up its mind whether it's rain, snow or good round hailstone. There had been ominous signs from October onwards. Gigantic geese barbs imprinted the skies from an early stage. The bigger the skeins the blacker the outlook or so the old people said. On blackthorn and white were superabundances of sloe and haw, sure auguries of stormy days ahead. All the time the moon, full and otherwise, was never without a shroud. Then came an awesome night in the middle of January. Before darkness fell cautionary ramparts of puce coloured, impenetrable cloud were seen to make dusty inroads into an ever-changing sky. The wind blew loudly and as night wore on it blew louder still.

At midnight a storm of unprecedented savagery ravaged the countryside. Wynds of hay were carried aloft and deposited in alien fields miles away. Trees were flattened and suspect haysheds gutted but of all the destructive acts perpetrated that night none was so capricious as that which swept the slates from the roof of Tom Fly-Low's bedroom. The rest of the house was left untouched. At half past one in the morning the oldest of the Fly-Low brothers found himself staring upwards into a swirling sky.

Wise man that he was he decided to stay abed till the storm spent itself. This it did as dawn broke mercifully over a devastated landscape.

After breakfast the brothers inspected the damage. Structurally there was nothing the matter. They came to the conclusion that a sufficiency of second-hand slates was all that was required to repair the roof. They knelt beside the kitchen fire and offered a Rosary in thanksgiving. Immediately after-

wards the youngest brother Jack was commissioned to under-
take the journey to the distant town of Listowel, there to forage
among the premises of builders' providers for the necessary
materials. Tom Fly-Low who acted as treasurer to the household counted fifty pounds in single notes into Jack's hands
while Billy went in search of the black mare. She would be
tackled to the brothers' only transport, a large common cart
with iron-banded wheels.

Jack shaved in the kitchen and changed into his Sunday
clothes. He dipped a brace of calloused fingers in the holy
water font which hung just inside the front door, made the
Sign of the Cross and went out of doors to begin the eleven
mile journey to the town. He was met in the cobbled yard by a
fuming Billy. The mare had broken from the stable during the
storm and was nowhere to be found. There was nothing for it
but to walk to town and hope for a lift.

After the second mile Jack stopped and lit his pipe. He sat
in the lee of a densely-ivied hedge and allowed himself a brief
rest. Around him the light green of well-grazed fields mottled
with dung-induced clumps of richer grass shone in the winter
sunlight. Birds sang in roadside bushes. Wearily he got to his
feet and continued on his journey. As he did an ancient Bed-
ford truck appeared around a bend at his rear. Before he had
time to hail it the drive had changed gears and brought it to a
halt. Jack Fly-Low climbed into the cab.

The driver was a thin-faced, refined-looking man wearing
a tattered black tam and faded overalls. After Jack had thanked
him there was silence for a mile or so.

'Don't I know you?' the driver asked.

'I don't see how you could,' Jack told him. 'I don't know
you.'

'My name is Florrie Feery,' the driver introduced himself.

'And my name is Jack Counihan,' Jack responded.

Half an hour passed without another word. At last they found themselves in the suburbs of Listowel.

'Where here do you want to be dropped off?' Florrie asked.

Jack Fly-Low mentioned the name of a prominent builders' provider, 'but,' said he, 'first I must stand you a drink.'

The first drink borrowed a second and a third at which stage they had taken possession of two seats near a small table in a cosy corner of the bar. A turf fire burned brightly in a fireplace nearby. When Florrie rose to order a fourth drink Jack protested. His business was pressing he explained. There was no time to spare.

'What can be so pressing?' Florrie asked, 'that won't keep till we've had a *deoch an dorais?*'

Instantly Jack felt ashamed. Here was this exceptional fellow who had picked him off the road when he might have been no more than a tramp or a common highwayman, who had asked for no reference when he opened the door of his cab, who only wanted to buy his round like any decent man. Over the fourth drink the conversation turned inwards on their personal business and respective families. Confidences were exchanged as a result of which Jack Fly-Low decided to divulge his reason for being in town. Florrie listened sympathetically and attentively.

'That's a coincidence,' he said half to himself, half to Jack, as soon as the latter had finished telling him about the disappearance of the slates.

'What is?' Jack asked.

'This chap near me back at home.'

'What about him?'

'Nothing ... except that he has an old house destined for demolition.'

'And?'

'And,' Florrie paused to sip his whiskey, 'on the top of his house is the finest roof of second-hand slates you or me is ever like to see.'

'It was God made our paths cross this morning,' Jack Fly-Low said solemnly. 'Do you think your man might be induced to sell the slates off this roof?'

Florrie permitted himself a deep chuckle. 'Only this morning he asked me if I would be on the look-out for a buyer.'

Thereafter they spoke in whispers at Florrie's insistence. There was the danger, he pointed out, that every Tom, Dick and Harry would get wind of the slates before he had time to close the deal on Jack's behalf. Caution, therefore, was of the essence. Because of his regard for Jack he would lay strong claim to a family relationship which existed between himself and the gentleman who owned the derelict house. He was of the opinion he could purchase and deliver the slates for a mere thirty pounds. Like a flash Jack Fly-Low's right hand went for his inside pocket. Florrie laid a restraining hand on his shoulder.

'Not here,' he said, 'let's go in the back.'

In the makeshift toilet at the rear of the premises the thirty pounds changed hands. A gentleman to the last Florrie insisted in handing back a pound in luck money. There were more drinks before the truck driver recalled that he had promised to purchase a load of turf in a distant townland. There was an emotional goodbye and a promise that the slates would be delivered not later than noon of the following Saturday.

It was close to midnight when Jack Fly-Low arrived home. Billy and Tom were waiting by the hearth for an account of the day's activities. They listened spellbound as the youngest brother recounted the details of the day's outing. They were particularly impressed with his account of Florrie. Jack regaled them with different facets of the man's character until well into the morning. Whenever he flagged he would be prodded or prompted by Tom or Billy. They longed for Saturday so that they might see this paragon for themselves.

Early on Saturday a tradesman arrived to ready the roof for the slating. By noon he was in a position to start work in earnest but as the day wore on there was no sign of Florrie.

'He'll come,' Jack told the others, 'just give him time.'

Every hour or so a mechanically propelled vehicle could be heard passing on the public road which passed by the extreme boundaries of the farm.

'Hush,' Jack would call, 'that's him now. That's him surely.' The faces of the three brothers would light up expectantly whenever the noise of an engine was borne upward by the breeze. The tradesman smiled slyly to himself. There was the making of a good story here he told himself, a tale that would bear telling in the pub that night. At five o'clock he departed. He promised to return the moment the slates arrived.

The days passed but there was no sign of Florrie. Weeks went by, then months. Daffodils arrived to brighten the spring fields. The thorn buds quickened in the hedgerows but of Florrie and the slates there was no sign.

From time to time the tradesman would call to enquire if the materials had arrived. He volunteered to cover the roof temporarily with corrugated iron but the brothers would not hear of this. What would Florrie think? They had convinced themselves that he had been taken ill or that he had been involved in a serious accident.

The brothers Fly-Low had implicit trust in Florrie. Had not Jack spent a day with him, vetted him from all angles so to speak and convinced himself that he was an uncommonly fine fellow. Summer came and went and Tom's room still lay exposed to the elements. He moved to a settle bed in the kitchen. The brothers were agreed that it would be a breach of faith if they made any attempt to cover the roof before Florrie arrived. Arrive he would. Of that they were certain.

Whenever neighbours called to pass the time of day one or other of the Fly-Low's would interrupt the conversation if the noise of traffic came from the roadway.

'Hush, hush,' they would caution, 'that could be Florrie with the slates.'

It never was. In the houses around the neighbouring countryside the whole business of the slates became something of a standing joke. Whenever a vehicle was heard passing some member of the household was sure to say: 'Hush, hush now. That's Florrie with the slates.'

For years it was a catch cry with younger folk ever on the alert for any form of diversion. It was without malice. No one would intentionally make fun of the Fly-Lows. They were good neighbours, deeply religious and charitable to a fault.

As the years rolled on mention of Florrie became rarer and rarer in the Fly-Low kitchen. At night when the boozing of a lorry was heard in the chimney the brothers would exchange hopeful looks but no word would pass between them. Of the three Jack felt the disappointment most keenly. The others had not known Florrie like he had. Occasionally they might be forced to suppress nagging doubts and suspicions but having known the man in question he was never so affected.

The way Jack saw it any number of things could have happened. He recalled that Florrie was liberal with his money. This would not have escaped the notice of the numerous bar denizens who prey upon decenter types. Perhaps by now his body lay decomposed in some bog-hole or dyke. It was more likely, however, that an accident was responsible for his non-appearance. He had taken more than his fair share of drink on that memorable occasion in Listowel. For all Jack Fly-Low knew the poor fellow could be dead and buried long since or maybe it was how he lost his memory. He had heard of cases where the memory failed altogether after excessive consumption of doubtful whiskey.

Anything was possible. Inevitably Tom and Billy decided the roof should be covered. Otherwise the entire house would suffer. As a concession slates were not used. Instead sheets of corrugated iron were hammered into place by the tradesman. The new roof was laid on in the spring. In the winter of that year Tom Fly-Low passed away having succumbed to a bout of pneumonia. His brothers were convinced that the corrugated-iron roof was responsible. They gave the room a wide berth after Tom's burial.

Then one windy night in the spring of the following year the distinct boozing of an oncoming lorry was heard in the chimney. From the increasing volume of the sound it was clear that it was heading for the house of the Fly-Lows. Jack and Billy rose together, their faces taut, not daring to breathe. His heart pounding Jack opened the front door. Outside was a lorry. A man was alighting from the cab. He was approaching the doorway.

'Is it Florrie?' the barely whispered question came from

Billy who stood at his brother's shoulder. The driver came nearer. Jack Fly-Low stood unmoving. Beside him Billy trembled uncontrollably. The driver was speaking: 'Is this Dinnegan's?'

'No,' Jack answered. 'Go back the way you came. Dinnegan's is the next turn on the right.'

The driver was squat, coarse and throaty. Florrie had been slender and tall, elegant almost. The driver re-entered his cab, reversed and drove off.

In the kitchen Billy Fly-Low slumped against the table. The excitement had been too much for him. Unable to support himself he fell to the floor. A strange, unearthly sound came from his throat. Jack knelt and whispered an act of contrition into his brother's ear.

Some months after the funeral a group of neighbours came to visit Jack Fly-Low. During the interval between the visit and the burial of Billy he had grown gaunt and feeble. The neighbours were concerned. It might be best if he sold the farm and moved to town where help would be at hand should any sudden misfortune befall him. No. He would never leave the old homestead. A housekeeper then? No. Why not let the farm? No. Jack Fly-Low was adamant. He would look after himself to the end. In spite of this the neighbours made an agreement between themselves that they would call regularly to see him.

The following December there came an unexpectedly heavy snow storm. A number of outlying houses were cut off for several days. Among these was the Fly-Low abode. As soon as the byroads were passable a neighbour made his way to the hillock. He found Jack in a sorry state. His breathing came irregularly and weakly. Often for long spells he would gasp for breath. The neighbour left hurriedly and found somebody to notify the priest and doctor. Quickly he returned and sat on the bedside holding Jack Fly-Low's hand while the numbered breaths grew fainter. The neighbour was relieved when at last he heard the sound of the priest's car in the driveway. Vainly Jack Fly-Low endeavoured to raise himself to a sitting position. His throat crackled but no words came. His lips moved but no sound issued forth.

'What is it Jack? What's the matter?' the neighbour asked anxiously.

Gathering the last vestiges of his vanishing strength Jack Fly-Low opened his mouth. 'Florrie,' he whispered triumphantly before falling back on his pillow. His body slackened, the lips sealed themselves again but now there was the semblance of a smile on the shrunken dead face.

3
GUARANTEED PURE

Willie Ramley came to Ireland for one purpose, to marry a virgin. In a New York tavern he had been informed by a man with a brogue as thick as a turnip that Ireland abounded in colleens of this calibre.

'How will I know she's a virgin?' Willie Ramley asked.

'You'll know,' the man with the brogue assured him.

'But how?' Willie Ramley persisted.

'Take my word for it,' the man with the brogue had said, 'when the time comes all will be revealed.' This had been the gist of the impartation.

Willie was halfway through his second month in Ireland and contrary to his expectations nothing whatever had been revealed. He had travelled far and wide but none of the girls he had encountered had appealed to him. The only one he had questioned regarding her virginity tagged him straight off with a right cross which would have done justice to a Golden Gloves middle-weight. He ruefully pondered the advice tendered by the man with the brogue.

'All will be revealed,' he had said. It had been late on Saint Patrick's night. The man with the brogue whose name he had forgotten was regarded as something of a seer by the other patrons of the tavern. They treated him with deference and placed double whiskies in front of him from time to time for no apparent reason other than to bask in his favour. Willie could not remember how the conversation had started. All he recalled was that he had babbled out the story of his life concluding with the latest and most tragic chapter which contained the sordid details of how his latest girlfriend had been two-timing him. The seer had placed a hand on his shoulder and looked him straight between the eyes. With the other hand he handed him an untouched glass of whiskey.

'Drink that,' he had said, 'and take note of what I tell you.'

Willie Ramley did as he was bade.

'You see before you,' said the seer, 'a man who was once in the same quandary as yourself. My face is wrinkled now and my hair is grey but I was a sparkling fellow once eager for love and living. These same grey hairs and wrinkles have been acquired at immense expense. They, therefore, give me the right to advise a young chap like yourself, not to pontificate mark you, but to advise.' Wiping a tear from his eye he handed Willie Ramley a second glass of whiskey.

'Wait,' Willie had said, 'let me buy you one.'

'No,' the seer had countered. 'All those who come bearing me drinks have availed of my sagacity at one time or another. Should you and I meet again and should my counsel have proved to be beneficial I will expect a whiskey or two by way of compensation but for the present please regard these drinks which you see before me as much yours as mine.'

Willie nodded in agreement not wishing to interrupt with facile thanks the verbal flow of this most gracious old gentleman.

'When I was your age,' the sage continued, 'I jumped into matrimony with the first good-looking girl I saw. As a consequence the union was a disaster. It lasted three weeks. I was married secondly within six months and when that failed after a shorter period I vowed never again to marry. Oh vain resolve. In no time at all I was married again. You see my dear boy I was a martyr to matrimony. Seven times in all I ventured into the matrimonial stakes and seven times I came a cropper.'

At this juncture Willie Ramley felt constrained to put in a short spake.

'I would marry only once,' he said.

The seer was about to utter a caustic comment but something in the young man's demeanour stayed him.

'I know how you feel,' he said, 'but marrying only once might not be so simple.'

'I realise that,' Willie told him, 'but I am determined to succeed.'

'Then,' said the sage placing his hand upon the young man's shoulder for the second time, 'you must be doubly careful.'

'Counsel me please,' Willie begged him. 'Counsel me I beseech you before the years catch up with me and I am left to languish alone.'

'This is what you must do,' the seer said with a solemnity which became the problem. 'You must betake yourself to Ireland from which sainted spot my mother, God rest her, emigrated to these less virtuous climes. She was truly an angel if ever there was one outside the sacred precincts of Heaven.' Here the seer paused to acknowledge receipt of a wholesome shot of whiskey from a grateful client.

'Because you are pure yourself,' the sage continued after he had sipped from the fresh bumper, 'you seek a creature of equal purity.'

Willie Ramley nodded eagerly. All his instincts firmly intimated that he had stumbled at last upon an authentic oracle.

'Do not,' said the sage, 'let yourself be carried away by the first pretty face nor by some coy damsel who will seem to be the answer to all your dreams. Be patient and the right girl will show herself. There will be something about her, something special that will set her apart from all others. This particular something will be as much in evidence as the nose on your very own face. It will be as clear as though it were stamped upon her back. Go now and keep your wits about you. Be continent in your ways and true to your ideal and she will make herself known to you in the manner in which I have indicated.'

So saying the sage lifted both hands in an elaborate flourish indicating that he had said all he was going to say. Willie Ramley departed the scene and for weeks was fully absorbed by all that he had been told. He finally resolved that there was nothing for it but to travel to Ireland and it was thus that he found himself after six weeks, as far from attaining to his aspiration as he had been when he first set foot on the green land of Erin. Now, with less than a fortnight's time remaining to him he began to grow anxious and despaired of ever achieving his goal. So we find him in this despondent mood seated on a turtóg of snipegrass overlooking the vast beach of Ballybunion on a bright afternoon in the month of June.

Overhead seagulls mewed in the scented seaside air whilst around the human race disported itself as though fine days were at a premium. Elders paddled in the shallow shorewater whilst young men ventured beyond their depth endeavouring to test the concern of those inshore females for whom they had a special eye. Toddlers toddled, back and forth to the tide. Small boys and girls breathlessly shaped castles of sand with shovel and bucket whilst a golden-skinned lifeguard lorded it over all who sported in his domain. In short it could be said that everybody was happy except Willie Ramley.

Tired of sitting in one place he decided to venture uptown

with a view to imbibing a cool drink in one of the resort's many excellent hostelries. As he dandered along idly kicking empty cigarette and matchboxes with newly-purchased sandals he was almost run down by a bus. Had it not been for the fact that a passer-by hollered an alarm he might well have been injured. He managed to catch the barest glimpse of his benefactress, a shy young female who immediately averted her not unpretty head the moment she found his gaze turned in her direction. For a moment he stood unresolved outside the door of a popular tavern. The words of the seer came drifting back to him. He decided to investigate further. The young lady was by now out of sight but it seemed to Willie that she was one of a party of females which had been on its way to the beach. He proceeded at a lively pace until he found the party once more within his ken. It consisted of five members. He followed at a discreet distance not wishing to overplay his hand and thus destroy his chances altogether. The party descended a stone stairway to where an array of ancient bathing boxes stood facing the shimmering sea. There followed some brief negotiations with the proprietor after which the five took possession of a similar number of the rust-wheeled wooden structures.

Willie Ramley carefully noted the box into which his Lady Fair had disappeared. There was nothing for it but to wait until she came out. A strange sensation began to assail him, a composition of excitement and expectancy. He guessed that the five were country folk. He deduced this from the way in which they had looked around and about when they arrived at their destination. It was also apparent from their simple apparel and the way they carried themselves that they were daughters of the soil. He had expected a chaste emergence from the bathing boxes but he was totally unprepared for the sight which met his eyes. Each of the five was decked out in a long shift which fell to the toes and which concealed all the shapeliness thereunder. The shifts were off-white in colour and the material lightweight. What Willie Ramley could not know was that these full-length costumes were the common bathing attire of the people of the countryside. Thrifty souls that they were these frugal females rarely visited emporiums for the material which went into the making of their underclothes and beach attire. The flour which was used for the making of the daily bread came, as a rule, in calico bags of one hundred and twelve pounds or one hundredweight. When the flour was used up the bags were thoroughly washed and dried. The textile was used to make shifts, slips and knickers not to mention football togs and bedclothes. While the numerous town and city people on the beach might regard the calico-clad countrywomen with some amusement they, nevertheless, refrained from showing it. This could well be because they themselves had only recently emerged from country backgrounds.

Despite the lack of design the shifts sat well on their owners as they moved in stately formation from bathing boxes to shore with their heads held high to show how little they cared about what others thought. Their leader was a formidable, mightily-busted lady of late middle years, tall and broad-shouldered with aquiline features and a bearing which suggested that she was capable of defending herself and her charges in the unlikely event of an attack. The others were younger by far, late teens or early twenties so that Willie could not be blamed for concluding that the matriarch was more than likely the mother of the four. They walked demurely behind her looking neither left nor right. The girl who had prevented Willie's collision with the bus brought up the rear and it was clear that under the shapeless shift there was a body as beautiful as the imagination could conjure up. Reaching the water they proceeded along its edge to a spot where no other human soul was in evidence. Here, prompted by the matron, the young ladies entered the sea and after much skipping, leaping and shrieking accustomed themselves to its cold but salving wavelets. Then, dutifully while the matron kept a lookout in the background, the four faced themselves to the distant horizon and lifting the fronts of their shifts liberally sprinkled the exposed part of the anatomy with handfuls of cleansing sea water. The matron herself did not enter the water at all, content in her role of mother hen, repelling the curious with the most intimidatory of looks and doughty of stances. As soon as the girls had finished they chastely lowered their shifts and turned their backs to the very same horizon. The first exercise was repeated until the matron was satisfied that each was adequately bathed. Mustering her charges in a single file she resumed her position at the head of the column. Proudly and gracefully they returned the way they had come. Willie Ramley decided to make a closer inspection. He strode seawards with what he hoped was a casual air, pouting his lips into an indifferent whistle, giving the impression that he was an innocent holidaymaker lost in a private world of his own. Warily he circled round the matriarch as she led her brood to the boxes. His aim was to keep pace with the group from the rear so that he could better observe the lady of his choice. As he neared completion of his arc their eyes met ever so fleetingly but in that split-second exchange he lost his heart irrevocably. Again he recalled the seer's advice, 'Do not let yourself be carried away by a pretty face.'

There was more, however, to this young lady than a pretty

face. Of that he was certain. He fell in behind and then he saw for the first time the word 'Sunrise' imprinted in faded red letters on the back of the shift. Willie Ramley would have had no way of knowing that this was the brand name of the popular variety of flour greatly favoured by the country folk of the time. The letters were in large capitals and underneath there was a longer inscription in faded black italics.

Anxious to acquaint himself with its contents he closed the gap between them until the lettering was easily legible. 'One hundred and twelve pounds,' it said, 'guaranteed pure.'

He repeated the words over and over again to himself but it was only when the object of his interest had disappeared into her bathing box that the full significance of the latter part of the seer's advice impressed itself upon him. What was that he had said again, something about a special mark or sign that would set his wife-to-be apart. But what were the precise words? Slowly they came back to him.

'There will be something about her ... It will be as clear as though it were stamped upon her back.' Those were the exact words as far as he could recall. No further evidence of the girl's character was needed. He waited impatiently for her re-emergence.

For the remainder of his holiday Willie Ramley embarked upon a consistent and most earnest suit. Morning, noon and night he waited upon her. The girl's mother was impressed by his undeviating devotion and when at length Willie had prevailed upon the young lady to say yes the mother approved unreservedly and the pair were married. The honeymoon, as was to be expected, was spent in Ballybunion and on the first night of what turned out to be a most blessed union the blushing bride presented herself to her husband clad in nothing but the long shift which carried on its back the inscription: 'One hundred and twelve pounds. Guaranteed pure.' And indeed it must be said here that never was a product so truthfully advertised.

4

'THE TEAPOTS ARE OUT'

'I was present,' Dinny Colman boasted, 'the day the first shot was fired.'

'It wasn't a shot was it?' my mother prompted, noticing my bewilderment.

'Of course it wasn't,' Dinny replied, 'but in all wars household or otherwise, someone has to start things off. The wrong word in the wrong place at the wrong time will do just as nicely or suppose people was taking their supper and if someone was to get fat meat who didn't like fat meat while others who didn't care whether they got fat or lean was presented with lean that would do it. I seen it happen. It may seem a small thing but in the eyes of the victim a great wrong has been done. A man's supper has been destroyed and in this God-forsaken countryside a man's supper is about the only diversion he has before drawing the clothes over his head for the night.'

He flicked the reins and called 'Giddap!' The bobbing rump twitched. The ears pricked. The paces stretched and quickened. The wind sang in our ears and we had to raise our voices to be heard. We were travelling on the flat. It wasn't till the pace slowed as we climbed the first of the forbidding hills on the road homeward that I found the composure to ponder Dinny's remarks.

The house we had just left was a thatched, one-storey farmhouse like our own. Indeed it was like every other farmhouse in the countryside with the difference that on the one we had lately vacated the thatch was hoary and rotten, retaining not a glimmer of the rich burnished yellow which it once boasted. The white-washed walls were long since brown-stained by the stinking, blackened rainwater which oozed and seeped from the reeking thatch. The small, deep-set windows afforded little or no light to the interior. Add to this the fact that they had not been cleaned for years save where the imprint of a palm had smoothed a lookout from which occasional visitors might be vetted. The run-down farm had been let year after year to a neighbour while the byroad from the main road to the house was no longer distinguishable from the rushy fields through which it ran. Famished, underfed bullocks stood waiting for hay in a large bawling herd just inside the main gate. They looked as if they hadn't eaten for days! The general picture was one of casual decay.

'The teapots was out when we landed and out when we left.' Dinny was speaking to my mother.

The farm was owned by Neddy Leary. With him in the kitchen during our visit had been his wife Dolly and his sister Bridgeen. Because they had been partaking of some afternoon tea we had surprised them. Each was seated at a different table, Neddy at the large, main table which stood in the centre of the kitchen, his wife and sister at either side of the turf fire which smouldered under a large, black iron kettle. Each had wet and drawn their separate pots of tea and withdrawn with them to their respective positions. Bread, milk, butter and sugar were communal and could be had from an appointed area at the end of the main table. The remaining space was restricted, the preserve of Neddy Leary. In truth the smaller tables were no more than glorified butter boxes which had been upturned and covered with patches of spare tarpaulin.

We had heard the sounds of discord quite plainly as we neared the house. All three were involved. It had reached hysterical proportions just as my mother knocked upon the door. Suddenly there wasn't a titter to be heard. A grimy face appeared at the window and shortly afterwards a voice called, 'Come in.' By this time, however, Dinny Colman, who was never a man to stand on ceremony, had the door open. The disarray was quite evident.

'God bless all here,' he used the benediction to camouflage his extreme curiosity. Hastily Dolly Leary and her sister-in-law Bridgeen departed the hearth clutching their teapots and other relevant accoutrements. They disappeared soundlessly into an adjacent room.

'Come in, come in,' Neddy Leary cried as though there had never been a word of disagreement. Dinny Colman made immediately for the hearth and stood with his back to it so that the whole kitchen could be kept more easily under observation.

'Servant boys don't know their place no more,' Neddy Leary addressed himself to my mother at the same time rising and ushering us both to the hearth where he bade us sit on the chairs which had just been abandoned. This left Dinny with no choice but to move to one side. Using heavy black tongs Neddy Leary set himself the task of re-arranging the turf fire. This he managed to do with a surprising degree of skill. In seconds it was a tastefully-constructed pile of glowing embers, quite pleasant to behold and radiating welcome warmth. He delicately banked it with sods chosen from an ancient tea-chest which stood nearby. He declined, however, to sweep the hearth and surrounds clean of ashes. He managed to give the impression that this was a chore beneath his dignity.

'As soon as that kettle boils,' he politely informed my mother, 'we'll wet a mouthful of tea and discuss your business.'

Having said this his face hardened and he called out in a loud voice, 'Come down here this instant.' As he once more turned to my mother the harshness left his face. 'They'll be down now to set the table,' he told her. Meanwhile Dinny Colman had moved nearer the door where he made a thorough investigation of that makeshift portal. He seemed determined to record every contrary detail. He moved next to the farthest corner overhead which was a hen-coop covered by lattice wire. Several pullets and hens of the Rhode Island Red species sat contentedly staring into space as though drugged or dazed. Reaching upward Dinny thrust a finger though the lattice and tapped the nearest of the hens on its beak. There followed a soft, fruity clucking.

'Let those hens be!' The order came from Neddy Leary. He had been noting Dinny's progress with mounting displeasure. Dinny moved on to where a picture of the Sacred Heart was barely visible through a cracked, dust-covered glass frame. He took a deep breath and expelled it in the direction of the picture. His every action was a deliberate manifestation of his amusement.

Dolly Leary was the first to arrive from the room. 'You know my woman don't you?' Neddy said.

'Indeed I do,' my mother answered. Nevertheless she shook hands with Dolly who looked far tidier now than when we first entered.

After a few moments, enough to allow Dolly establish herself, Bridgeen Leary presented herself. 'And my sister,' Neddy said. Again there was a handshake.

'Will ye take an egg with the tea?' Neddy enquired and he lifted a black canister with the tongs. It was half-filled with murky water the surface of which was partly covered with ashes.

'No thanks,' the three of us answered hastily, too hastily. My mother made amends by stating that we had partaken of our dinners just before we set out. Dolly and Bridgeen began to clear the table. They were watched closely by Dinny who had returned to resume a less familiar form of communication with the Rhode Island Reds. Between them the women of the house managed to spirit away all the unsightly objects which had first greeted us. In no time at all a tablecloth covered the table. There were cups and saucers, side plates and a large dish which contained an outsize pancake and the quarter of a currant loaf.

'Dang that kettle,' Neddy Leary said but just as he spoke the faint curling steam from its spout was suddenly transformed into a solid jet. He took himself to the table where a whispered consultation took place between himself and the two women. The argument concerned itself with which of the three teapots should be used for the occasion. One word borrowed another and it seemed as if the parley might erupt into a major row. Suddenly there was silence. An agreement had been reached. Dolly Leary raced to the room she had just left and returned at once with a brown earthenware teapot which was obviously being pressed into service for the first time. It was quickly rinsed with a gurgling squirt from the boiling kettle. Neddy arranged a circle of small coals of a uniform size a few inches from the fire and on these the freshly-made tea in its brand new teapot was allowed to draw.

While we waited Dolly and Bridgeen made the joint observation that I was like my father but had my mother's eyes. Meanwhile in the hen-coop there was uproar. Dinny, the party responsible, had quickly removed himself from the scene of the crime and was once again inspecting the door.

'Take a seat at once sir,' Neddy spoke curtly and indicated a chair at the bottom of the table. Suspecting that a limit might have been reached Dinny sat at once. One by one we joined him at the table. Neither of the household women sat till the tea had been poured. Neddy sliced the pancake and the currant loaf. A tell-tale, off-white vein ran through each of the pancake slices. In the case of the currant loaf the fruit had sunk to the bottom. Despite this we would be obliged to partake of at least one slice. Thereafter it would be possible to decline all pressure to eat more. Gingerly we opted for the currant loaf. It was heavy going. No crumb fell to the table or the floor such was its soggy consistency. We managed to get it down, however, and so placed ourselves in a position to refuse all other offers. The household, having satisfied itself that our wants were fulfilled, ate heartily until nothing remained in the dish.

'Now,' Neddy Leary announced as he wiped his mouth with the back of his hand, 'tell us what it was that brought ye.'

'Not much,' my mother answered, 'just to find out if you could give us your brother Tom's address in New York.'

'With a heart and a half but tell us who belonging to you is for America?'

'This boy here,' my mother informed him.

'He's young isn't he?'

'Old enough at sixteen,' my mother responded.

Neddy Leary sighed. 'The best age,' he agreed. 'They don't settle so well when they shove on in the years. That was Tom's age when he left. Never looked back. Made out fine for himself.'

Neddy's younger brother Tom figured as a sort of intercessory between prospective American employers and the droves of young Irish boys and girls who emigrated yearly from the district. It was a genuine labour of love on his behalf and indeed it would be unthinkable for any intending emigrant not to contact him before leaving. His house served as a home from home during those heartbreaking first weeks. It gave the youngsters a chance to absorb the strange, complex environment until such time as they were able to make some slight evaluation of the new situation for themselves.

'I'll get it for you right away,' Neddy said. He rose and entered another room to the left of the kitchen. Nobody spoke during his absence. My mother cleared her throat and was about to say something but changed her mind. Dinny Colman eased himself self-consciously out of his chair and betook himself to the hearth where he first looked up the sooty chimney before standing with his behind to the fire, hands behind his back. He stood with a knowing smile on his face, his lips pursed, issuing a sly, soundless whistle. Neddy returned with a writing pad, a bottle of black ink and a small well-thumbed notebook. Behind his ear was a wooden-handled pen with a rusty nib. His wife and sister cleared the table feverishly while he stood imperiously waiting behind his chair. His eyes scanned the table for signs of any object which might impair the work which was about to begin. When he sat the two women stood in attendance directly behind him no more than a foot apart. Even Dinny Colman was impressed by the ritual. He was made to feel that he was in the presence of a scribe. An inner sense told him that it was not a moment for levity. Laboriously Neddy Leary laid out his writing materials on the table. When he was settled properly in his chair he uncorked the ink bottle, having first held it up to the light for careful inspection in case it harboured any foreign bodies. Satisfying himself in this respect he next inspected the rusty nib. Not finding it to his satisfaction he thrust it into his mouth, twirling it round and round several times therein and then proceeded to suck it as though it were a lollipop. Removing it he held it close to his eyes for final inspection. He dried it by the simple expedient of rubbing it against the sleeve of his coat. He then wet the thumb of his right hand with his tongue, lifted the notebook eye-high and thumbed through its tattered pages until a deep sigh of satisfaction intimated that he had found what he had been looking for.

'Thomas Ignatious Augustine Leary,' he chanted the words with due solemnity. 'Two forty-seven, East Two Sixty-second Street, City of New York, United States of America', he concluded with an American twang. He then carefully proceeded to copy the address onto the notepaper. As he wrote not a pin could be heard to fall, a feather to alight, a heart to flutter, until he had almost completed his task. Quite out of the blue, you might say almost sacrilegiously, his sister Bridgeen covered part of her bosom with one hand and all of her mouth with the other before emitting a clearly audible gasp that shattered the concentration of the scribe as though a shotgun had been discharged over his head. His reaction was not to erupt from his chair mouthing blasphemous barrages in his sister's direction. He merely folded his hands while the colour of his face changed to a ghastly hue. A nerve-jangling silence of several moments ensued. Neddy Leary closed his eyes and spoke.

46

'Is there somebody present with something to say?' His voice shook with emotion. It was evident that he was making mighty efforts to control himself.

'It was me made the noise,' Bridgeen replied without a hint of apology in her voice.

'Why so?' Neddy was now drumming his fingers inquisitorially on the table.

'Because,' said his sister sarcastically, 'that's the old address.' So flaring a transgression was this that it simply had to be ignored. To contradict the head of the house in the presence of strangers could not be brooked no matter what. In the circumstances the only alternative was to pretend the woman had not spoken. Without haste Neddy finished off the address, rose, held it to the fire and allowed the ink thereon to dry. While he was thus engaged his wife committed the second cardinal error of the afternoon.

'If you're not careful you'll burn it,' she said. From the expression on his face it was plain that Neddy had decided to treat this comment with the same detachment as the other. When the ink had dried he folded the sheet of notepaper and handed it to my mother. His hands trembled and a furious fire burned in his dark eyes.

'I wish the boy luck,' he said gently, 'and now if you have no further business you might like to be shortening your road.'

'Of course,' my mother agreed, 'and let me thank you for your kindness.'

A sensitive woman she could readily presage the signs of the approaching storm. Any moment now the lightning would flash and the thunder roll and crack. The barely restrained winds of rage were already rustling dangerously. One could almost run one's fingers over the bristling tension.

'Time to go,' my mother ushered me to the door which Neddy Leary had obligingly opened for us. As ever Dinny Colman was inclined to dawdle. He posed affectedly in the doorway as though admiring the landscape while all he really wanted was to savour the beginnings of the oncoming conflict. He savoured it all right but not in the manner he would have liked. Behind him stood Neddy Leary waiting to close the door so that he might give rein to his anger. When Dinny refused to budge Neddy drew back his right foot and forcefully impressed the side of his boot on Dinny's buttocks making him to buck forward unceremoniously till he found himself on all fours. As soon as the kick was implanted Neddy banged the door shut, the better to begin the domestic dissension in earnest. Outside, after Dinny had recovered, we marvelled at the indoor commotion. The first shot was fired in this instance when the ink bottle came flying through the window. Then came the clangour of human voices upraised and distorted till they seemed inhuman. It was a wanton, reckless, irascible strife. There was the sound of splintering wood mingled with the crash of breaking crockery. Add to this the noisome jangle of canisters, pannies, buckets and other tin missiles and some idea of the general bedlam will be conveyed.

The climax came with a mighty crash followed by the terrified clucking of badly-maimed hens. The hen-coop had fallen; whether by accident or design we could not determine. Suddenly there was silence. The battle was over. The door opened and a file of Rhode Islanders staggered and limped out from the scene of the fray. In the kitchen Neddy Leary sat at the table with his head in his hands. His wife and sister sat holding their sides at either side of the hearth. A lifeless hen lay sprawled on the floor. There was debris everywhere.

'Come along,' my mother said, 'they'll need to be alone now.'

'The teapots will be out forever after this,' Dinny Colman forecasted. He was still peeved at the way he had been treated by Neddy Leary. Reluctantly he followed us to the pony and trap. As we climbed the second hill Dinny was still muttering to himself over the injustice which had been done to him.

'Tell us about the very first shot,' I said. He mulled over the suggestion for a while.

'I worked there at the time,' he began. 'It was a fine place, carrying twenty milch cows and two score of dry stock. There was only the pair of them, Neddy and the sister. Tom had gone to the States to make his fortune. Neddy one night took it into his head to carry Dolly Mack home from a dance in the village. He made a habit of the thing after that and it was no time at all before the pair decided to marry. The trouble started the second day after the marriage. We were after coming in from the meadow. The new wife laid the table and put the eggs on to boil. Bridgeen sat near the fire darning a sock. Things was quiet and peaceful.

'Will you eat one egg or two?' Dolly asked of Neddy.

'Two if you please,' said he.

'Will you eat one egg or two?' she says to me.

'Two if you please,' said I.

'Will you eat one egg or two?' she says to Bridgeen Leary, her sister-in-law.

'Will I eat my own eggs is it?' she threw back at Dolly. That was the first shot to be fired between the two and of course Neddy was soon drawn into it. The teapots came out soon after that and from the looks of things today they'll stay out for all time.'

5
UNDER THE SYCAMORE TREE

Jimmy Bowen was by no means fastidious, yet every evening he would shave and wash meticulously before donning his best clothes in preparation for his trip to the river side. Having left the house he would stand in front of the shop window and take careful stock of himself. Should there be the slightest evidence of disorder anywhere on his person he would re-enter the house straightaway and set about correcting the imperfection. Having satisfied himself that every possible step had been taken regarding the reorganisation of his appearance he would present himself a second time to the shop window. Often he would stand there for several minutes pretending to be engrossed in a study of the window's contents whereas he was really searching for flaws in his appearance. When he was satisfied that no further improvement could be effected he would set off on his walk. The time he chose varied from season to season but always it would be roughly a half hour before darkness fell. First he would stroll leisurely through the streets before arriving at the laneway which led to the river side path. The moment he sighted the water his features underwent a change. His eyes grew brighter. His ears seemed to prick as though he were alerting himself for an exciting encounter. He became a different person.

At sixty Jimmy Bowen was a spare, grey-haired, lively man who moved with an athlete's facility. He was well off. Rumour had it that he never married because the girl he loved was killed in a car accident or drowned or worse. Nobody was quite clear. He had left the town in his late teens and returned twenty years later to take over the family hardware business when his father was taken ill. He had never seen eye to eye with the old man although they had never lost touch or so it was said. When the elder Bowen died Jimmy assumed control. His mother passed on shortly afterwards and it seemed inevitable that he would take a wife. He was young enough. A fit man of forty with his reputed means should have no trouble. He remained single, however, and was the bane of the town's over-blossomed spinsters for several years. At sixty with his hair whitened by the years he was no longer regarded as a candidate for the marriage stakes. His business prospered and there was much conjecture as to what would happen when he grew too old to carry on. He had a first cousin in a distant town, a ne'er-do-well with a large brood. Jimmy was persuaded by friends of the family that it would be an act of charity to bring the oldest boy into the business. It hadn't worked. The lad knew it all from the outset. He disappeared one day with several hundred pounds and was heard of no more.

The river side path which was the route of Jimmy's evening strolls was flanked on the one side by giant oaks and sycamores and on the other by the wide sweep of the river bank. It was a picturesque walk less frequented now than at any time in its history. Lovers no longer dallied there preferring to speed through the countryside in motor cars. Older people, unless the weather was exceptionally fine, chose to sit and watch television. Consequently the only people Jimmy Bowen met were the occasional fowler and fisherman. This was the way he liked it even though it must be said that he entertained other secret aspirations. His favourite time was when darkness descended. To celebrate this delicate event he would stand unmoving under a favourite sycamore. It was best when no breezes blew. On these occasions of tranquillity he would stand entranced, utterly absorbed by what was happening. Sometimes the motionless lineaments of the river would be mottled with infinitesimal flecks of foam. Even the birds would be hushed. It would be that precise time of evening when light resigns itself to half light yielding finally to darkness and it seemed all nature was aware that consummate stillness was required if an honourable surrender was to take place. This was the very time when Jimmy Bowen longed for fulfilment of his secret aspirations. Quite simply what he hoped for was that a woman, the woman of his dreams, might emerge from the river side shadows and stand by his side to share in the romantic transition. It was, he knew, more than he was entitled to expect in such a place and at such a time. When as always she failed to materialise he would return the way he had come still cherishing the notion that she might appear before him out of one of the many bowers and groves along the way. At the back of his mind was the certainty that she would appear one evening. She would just happen to be there and that would be that. When it happened he would take her hand and they would return together towards the lights of the town. Words would be unnecessary.

The cold truth was that for twenty years Jimmy had returned to the town empty-handed but this had not succeeded in putting a damper on his expectations. He was as hopeful as ever. In the shop he worked with such earnest endeavour that no onlooker could possibly credit that the man's private life was founded on such improbable romantic notions. The very opposite would seem to be far more likely. His staff consisted of two counter-hands, middle-aged brothers who had started their apprenticeships with his father. There was a federal factotum, an elderly fellow, another relict from his father's tenure and there was Miss Miller. It would be difficult to determine Miss Miller's exact age. Mousy Miller the customers called her. She had joined the staff at the time of his father's illness and spent her working hours in an elevated glass office where she could command a view of every corner of the shop. She dressed chastely, wore spectacles and rarely used make-up. She had few friends and seemed content to spend most of her free time with her landlady, an elderly widow. Originally she hailed from the midlands. Her people, it was believed, were modest farmers. Jimmy rarely entered the office. When he did it was at Miss Miller's invitation. She always stood when he entered and allowed him to take the seat which she had just vacated. Usually the visit would consist of inspecting a contractor's account which might have exceeded the stipulated limit or to discuss the necessity for consulting a solicitor over other unpaid accounts of long standing. She always called him Mr Bowen. He never called her anything but Miss Miller. Although he never objected to these occasional conferences he always felt that his presence was superfluous. She might appear to be mousy and effete but her knowledge of the business was astonishingly comprehensive. The books were immaculately kept. At a moment's notice she could provide an exact rundown of the firm's financial standing for any period. It was she who dealt with the auditors, saw to the stocktaking and staff bonuses, made up the weekly wage packets and took on the hundred and one other minor tasks which contributed to the running of a successful business. It could be said that she knew her employer inside out. Jimmy knew her worth and paid her accordingly. Ask anywhere in the town and you would be told that, whatever else, Jimmy Bowen was first and foremost a decent man.

He had a somewhat different relationship with the rest of the staff. A casual customer would be hard put to know who was boss and who was counterhand. It worked well. The country people who patronised the shop liked a man without pretension, a man who would sit on the counter and pass the time of day. He had other traits which appealed to townspeople and country people alike. The chief of these was his tendency to take off on the occasional skite. He never took a conventional holiday. When the urge caught him, an urge which generally coincided with a fine spell, he would betake himself to the office pay slot and indicate his financial requirements to Miss Miller.

'Slip us a few hundred,' he might say. The money, in fivers and tenners, would be forthcoming at once without comment of any kind from Miss Miller.

'See you in a few days,' he would say as soon as the notes were pocketed. Home then to change into slacks, pullover and sandals. Garage next for a petrol fill and a hasty check of elementals. Thence to the nearest city or, if the season was right, to a distant holiday resort. His customers received news of these breaks with amusement. They knew the drill or thought they did. There had to be a woman or women. Why else would he go on his own? A good man's case this. Not even a stepmother would blame him. Many envied him the manner in which he took off in the first place. He needed nobody's permission and best of all he could come back when it suited him. On his return he never tendered the least information as to how he had fared, a sure sign, this his friends said, that a debauch had taken place.

The truth was that Jimmy Bowen did no more than sleep out in the mornings. The remainder of the day he spent inspecting the neighbourhood pubs and hotels. Sometimes he drank on his own. Other times he joined up with single gentleman like himself or became involved in sing-songs. By midnight it would be as much as he could do to locate his room under his own steam. This then was the pattern of his respite. There had never been any serious involvement with a woman. He remained faithful to his river side fantasies and would fall into a happy if drunken sleep recalling the enchanting images of his favourite place or endeavouring to trace the shadowy features of the lovely creature who had thus far failed to realise herself from the place in question. Always he slept soundly, not waking till the chambermaids knocked on his door at a time when the morning was well advanced. He never surfaced before noon. By the time he had read through the morning papers lunch would have become available. Having partaken he would sit for a while before indulging in the only physical exercise of the day. This consisted of an hour long stroll after which he felt free to indulge himself in the first drink of the day. After a sojourn of four to five days his appetite for change would be sated and he would return home. There would be no drink on the day of the homecoming. He also made a point of arriving at the shop after dark. After a snack he would make straight for his bed where he stayed until the effects of the prolonged booze had worn off. As a rule this took no more than a sleep out until the late afternoon of the following day when he would arise refreshed and ready to resume his normal way of life. This was not to say that he was abstemious between skites. Most nights after returning from the river he stopped off at the Anglers' Rest where he allowed himself a whiskey or two before polishing off a few pints of draught stout. He never drank alone. There was always a crony or two in attendance and invariably he joined up with these until time was called.

Shortly after his sixtieth birthday he embarked upon the longest and most intensive skite of his career. He departed the town early on Monday afternoon and was not seen again in its vicinity for a period of ten days. What transpired during that time will never be fully revealed. Even with the aid of Miss Miller, if Jimmy Bowen ever endeavoured to itemise the events which took place, the task would be impossible for the excellent reason that they were beyond recall. To be more accurate it could be said that they had foundered irrevocably in an alcoholic haze. Occasionally in later years glimpses of that foggy interlude would be borne back to him but none of sufficient duration or clarity to enlighten him. It was, as he intimated to his cronies not long after his return, the father and mother of all skites and the cronies to give them their due accepted this evaluation without question. Jimmy Bowen was not a man to exaggerate. There was no doubt that he had been on the skite of a lifetime. What he did remember most vividly at that, was waking up on the final day. His head throbbed with a pain so over-powering that he despaired of ever facing the world again. For hours he tossed and turned on the bed. Towards late afternoon he steeled himself with every ounce of resolve at his disposal and entered the bathroom. He filled the bath with cold water and stood nearby in his pelt waiting for it to fill. This will kill me or cure me he told himself. He did not ease himself into the water. It might be said that he plopped in.

He screamed when the first shock assailed him. Having barely survived it he shuddered and spluttered like a man demented as the cold touched every part of his body. Despairingly he started to sing. His voice trembled and shook. He could not sustain a single note no matter how hard he tried. There was one fearful moment when he felt totally paralysed. Panic-stricken he erupted from the bath and landed on his behind on the slippery floor. Raising laboriously he dried himself thoroughly. After a few minutes he felt an improvement. His head still throbbed but the pain was now bearable. His hands were steady. He decided to risk a shave. Surprisingly he negotiated the business without a nick. He combed his hair and sat on the bed. He had no idea where he was. He was about to lift the phone when it occurred to him that he was naked. Hastily he pulled on his trousers. There was still some money in the fob; he was surprised at the amount. Probably cashed a cheque or two. All would be revealed in due course as the man said. He lifted the receiver and waited.

'Good afternoon, Mister Bowen.'

'Good afternoon. Where am I?'

A hearty girlish laugh from the other end.

'I'm serious. Where am I?'

'Poor Mister Bowen. I believe you.'

'Well?'

'The Neptune.'

'Galway?'

'Galway.'

'Thanks.' There was relief in his voice. Galway was less than three hours from home. He looked at his watch. Three forty-five. First he would eat something, pay his bill and then the road. He estimated that a leisurely speed should see him safely home with plenty of light in hand. He looked forward eagerly to the drive. At seven-thirty as he drove through the outskirts of his home town there was still no sign of darkness. Like the skite which he had just put behind him he would never be able to present a detailed or coherent account of what happened next. He decided that it was too bright to go straight to the shop. Instead he headed for the Angler's Rest. The place was deserted save for the proprietress Mrs Malone.

'You're back,' she said as though he had been away no longer than usual. There had in fact been mounting speculation all the week about his whereabouts. This had been replaced by genuine concern. In fact his cronies had decided to take the matter up with the civic guards should he fail to show up at the weekend. A skite was a skite but there were limits.

'Did you have a nice time?' Mrs Malone asked, hoping that the excitement did not show in her voice.

'Tip top,' Jimmy assured her. 'Let's have a glass of Jameson will you?'

While she dispensed the order Mrs Malone considered which of Jimmy's cronies and which of her own friends she would ring first. Collecting the note which he had tendered she excused herself, ostensibly to look for change. She made several phone calls, at the same time keeping an eye on Jimmy from the back lounge where the phone was located. She conveyed each individual disclosure in a tone that was little above a whisper. Jimmy sat silently sipping his whiskey unaware of what was going on. It had not occurred to him that his prolonged absence might have generated disquiet. All his thoughts were concentrated in an effort to determine the rate at which the daylight was fading outside.

'All too soon,' he told himself, 'it will be dark.' Suddenly

58

he rose. He had reached a decision. It was time for his visit to the river. The whiskey had left him groggy but it had also brought a welcome warmth. In this happy state he departed the Anglers' Rest and sauntered, at leisure, to the river side. Twilight hung between the river and the sky. In all too short a time darkness would envelop the scene and the magical fleeting moments of transition would be no more. Already the shadows were expanded to their fullest. Any moment now the last pale threads of evening would vanish into the dark tapestry of night. Jimmy Bowen proceeded apace towards his favourite tree. The world stood still or so it seemed. The mottled water moved soundlessly on. Jimmy Bowen stopped, arrested in his tracks by what seemed to be a female form standing under the wide branches of the sycamore. His heart fluttered. His breathing quickened. He peered prayerfully through the half-light, advancing slowly. There was no mistaking the form. It was definitely that of a woman. A flimsy headscarf adorned her averted head. A white mackintosh covered her slender frame. This cannot be, Jimmy Bowen told himself and yet the creature is there, living and breathing as sure as darkness is descending. He harrumphed delicately lest he startle her. She turned suddenly and in a thrice she was in his arms. All at once Jimmy Bowen knew that something huge, something altogether monumental had been missing from his life until that moment. The embrace lasted an eternity or so Jimmy thought. In reality it ended after half a minute. He dared not look at her face. He risked a hasty glance and was pleased with what he saw in the darkness. Her features were somewhat angular but pleasantly defined. A solitary tear or what he took to be a tear glistened on her cheek under the weak moonlight. This was to be expected. They had both waited for too long a time. He was equally overcome even if there was no tear to prove it. Gently he took her by a hand that melted immediately into his. Slowly they returned along the way he had come. Mrs Malone looked up apprehensively when the door opened. She always did. A pub was a pub and you never knew when a troublemaker might put in an appearance. The relief showed on her face when Jimmy Bowen entered. This was wiped away altogether and replaced by genuine amazement when she beheld his companion.

'Sweet, Sacred heart,' she addressed her customers, ''tis Mousy Miller and she without her specs.'

All within earshot turned to stare. A hush fell over the bar. Mrs Malone allowed her eyes to focus on Jimmy Bowen. There was a sort of glow to him. He still stood beside the doorway in a total trance, Miss Miller by his side. It was as though they were waiting for somebody to direct them. There was a word somewhere for the way Jimmy Bowen looked. Mrs Malone could not bring it to mind at once. Moonstruck, that was it, moonstruck.

After a while one of Jimmy's cronies arose and located seats for the pair.

'I declare but she looks downright attractive,' Mrs Malone confided to the customer nearest her. 'A bit too much make-up maybe but, still and for all, attractive. You'd hardly know her.'

At the counter Jimmy dawdled happily for a moment or two.

'I'll have a Jameson,' he said.

'And Miss Miller?' Mrs Malone put the question.

'Miss Miller?'

'Behind you.'

Jimmy Bowen turned slowly and directed all his fading

60

energies towards a hard look at his companion.

'Dammit if she isn't a dead ringer for Miss Miller.' He threw the observation over his shoulder to Mrs Malone.

'Ask her what she's having.' Mrs Malone's exasperation was beginning to show. Still Jimmy refused to budge. He just stood there with his back to the counter, happily if perplexedly contemplating his new-found love.

'What are you having, dear?' Mrs Malone called.

'Sweet sherry if you please,' came the demure and immediate reply.

'Dammit if she don't talk like her as well.' For the first time a note of alarm registered in Jimmy's voice. It conveyed itself immediately to Miss Miller. She looked about shamefacedly.

'Dammit,' Jimmy Bowen was saying as he looked at her from another angle, 'it is Miss Miller. Why didn't somebody tell me?' He looked foolishly from one watching face to another. An awesome silence had descended. Everybody looked everywhere, at Jimmy Bowen and Mrs Malone, at one another, at the ceiling, everywhere but at Miss Miller.

'Excuse me,' it was no more than a whisper but it was heard in every corner of the bar. It came from Miss Miller. She was on her feet.

'Your sherry.' Mrs Malone proffered the offering too late. Miss Miller was already on her way to the door which she closed gently behind her. There followed a short period of uneasy silence. Then came the clamour of relief. Everyone spoke at the same time. Jimmy Bowen alone was silent. He seemed dumbfounded. On his face was a look of utter perplexity. Still reeling he walked slowly towards the door. For an hour or more he walked aimlessly through the streets. Slowly, painfully, sobriety returned to him. Eventually he found himself at his own shop window. He fumbled for his keys while he took stock of his reflection He looked none the worse for wear, eyes a little tell-tale maybe, face a little drawn, white hair a little tousled yet, all in all, presentable enough. He located the appropriate key but could not bring himself to insert it in the lock. He stood undecided, weighing the keys in his palm, considering his reflection. He closed his eyes firmly and opened them again. This time he looked beyond the reflection. Slowly in his mind a hazy background of trees and river water began to take shape. Out of the darkening landscape a pair of human forms, male and female, their features as yet indiscernible, emerged side by side from the shadows and stood under the sycamore. Jimmy Bowen held his breath as the female form gracefully inclined its head in his direction. The radiant smile on Miss Miller's face was for Jimmy Bowen and Jimmy Bowen alone. This was beyond dispute. Her heart showed clearly on her face. It sang for Jimmy Bowen.

'Why not?' he asked aloud. 'Why not?' he asked turning from the window and addressing himself to the street at large. 'Why not?' he asked of the stars overhead, 'why not, why not, why not?' he asked as he hastened to the widow's house where Miss Miller sat inside her window with a tear in her eye.

6
THRIFT

It was his father's miserliness that killed John Cutler. That's what the neighbours said afterwards. That was what Mick Kelly the postman said and Mick knew the Cutlers better than anybody. His cottage stood at the entrance to their farm. When John Cutler reached his thirty-fifth year he confronted his father with the fact that he was at the halfway stage in his life's span with nothing to show for it.

'A few more years,' he complained, 'and I'll be an old man.'

His father nodded but did not otherwise commit himself.

'I have a notion of getting married.' He threw the bait out hopefully but the older man refused to rise to it.

While John stood waiting for some expression of sympathy or approval his mother entered the kitchen. At once she sensed there was a showdown in progress. She busied herself by the fireplace silently praying that her industry would exempt her from taking sides.

'What do you expect me to do?' Tom Cutler rose from his chair and went to the open door where he absently surveyed the distant hills.

'You could sign over the place,' John suggested.

'Can't do that. Damn well you know I can't do that.'

'But why not?'

'Why not he asks and he knowing well. What's to become of your mother and me if you bring another woman in here?'

'Ye can have a room.'

'A room eh! A whole room to ourselves! And what about our feeding and a bit of money?'

'There will be guarantees in the agreement. The solicitor will see to that.'

'And will the solicitor be here every day to see that the guarantees are carried out? There is no way I would allow another woman in here without five thousand pounds. I'd also want a separate dwelling on the land, nothing fancy, mind you, just a simple cot for two. That's not asking a lot now is it?'

John threw his hands upwards in a gesture of total despair. 'Where would I get five thousand pounds,' he cried out angrily, 'and the money to build a house?'

'If your future wife had a fortune it would help.'

'My future wife as you call her has no money.'

'You could borrow,' the old man said.

'I couldn't,' John told him, 'not that kind of money; a few thousand yes but not what you ask.'

Tom Cutler shrugged his shoulders. 'It's tough,' he said, 'but I have to think of myself and your mother. If I don't nobody else will. That's been proved a thousand times over. Now if you've finished you might do down and turn in the cows.'

'So that's to be the end of it is it? My future is on the line and you want me to turn in the cows. Have you no more to say to me?'

'What more is there to say except that you have yourself to thank for the way you are today.'

'Myself to thank!' the words exploded from John's mouth.

'Oh now face up to the truth my boy. You didn't miss a night in the pub these last fifteen years.'

'Oh come off it,' John shouted. 'A few pints was the most I ever had and the beggars on the road had that.'

'A few pints every night,' his father pointed out, 'is a lot of pints come the end of the week. A thrifty man would have a nice pile put by at this time of his life.'

'What could I put by out of the miserable few pounds you paid me? After a packet of cigarettes and a drink there was nothing left. Nothing.' He spat out the words and brushed by his father with clenched fists.

'Drink and cigarettes, sure recipes for poverty,' the old man flung the words after him like stones after a worthless hound. He stood silently for a long while in the doorway. Then he turned to his wife.

'What do you make of that?' he asked. They were a wizened pair, looking older by far than their years. Both had sallow, pinched faces, stooped frames and decaying teeth. They presented an overall picture of neglect and want.

'I don't know what to say,' Minnie Cutler responded.

Tom shook his head at the outrageousness of it all.

'Do you think he has a woman itself?' he asked.

'I don't think so,' she answered after a while, 'leastways not a regular one.'

'I thought as much. All he wants is to get his hands on the place then drink it out.'

'Maybe if you were to give it over to him he'd come by a woman. No one will take with him unless the place is his own.'

'I can't do that. We both know it won't work.'

'But we have enough Tom. God knows how much you have in the banks.'

'You couldn't have enough for this world you foolish woman. When I go the place will be his but till that time he'll draw his wage and dance to my tune. I broke my back for this place and so did you. He'll bide his time.'

'I don't know Tom.' Minnie Cutler folded her arms. 'He's thirty-five. He's going to seed. Most men of his age have their own places or at least they have the handling of the money.'

'It won't work Minnie,' Tom Cutler was adamant. 'Look around you. Look what happened to them that signed over.'

'Some have it good Tom.'

'God's sake woman will you not be codding yourself. They're only letting on to have it good. Most of them are prisoners in the homes they once owned.'

'But isn't that the whole cause of the trouble Tom? Those that bought houses in the town or rented rooms are content enough. It's only when you have two women under the one roof that the trouble starts.'

'Do you want me to spend every penny I possess on a house. Is that it?'

'It needn't be big.'

'Of course it needn't be big but the money will be big and we'll end up paupers depending on a daughter-in-law for handouts.'

'If you signed over we'd have our old age pensions.'

'Will you get it into your head woman that I will not sign over. Do you think I'm mad. You want me to part with all I have in this world with one stroke of a pen.'

'You could go halves with him.'

'Won't work. The place isn't big enough to support two families.'

'Would you not tell him that you'd be prepared to sign over after a year or two?'

'No I would not, nor after twenty years if I live that long. There's a bit of a want in that fellow. He's a man for the good times. All he wants is drink and fags and carousing.'

'Still he's a good worker.'

'Is he now and pray how do you think he'd fare without me managing the place?'

'A woman would manage it for him quick enough.'

'This place calls for a thrifty man, a man that won't squander money foolishly. Let him wait. He'll appreciate it all the more when 'tis his. I'm away to the cows.'

'Who's to say but you're right,' Minnie Cutler conceded. Experience had taught her that it was prudent to concede ground which she knew she could not win anyway. Consequently there was never conflict between them, at least not of late.

For years too she had not mentioned his tight-fistedness. She took it for granted. According to him there was never anything to spare for clothes or holidays or titbits. He would always provide enough for the bare necessities but nothing more. In time she had stopped asking. It made for a peaceful atmosphere and in her estimation that was worth all the deprivation. Waste not want not had been Tom Cutler's strategy from the day he assumed ownership of the farm. It had been heavily in debt. Minnie's modest fortune had not been enough to compensate but non-stop penny-pinching had. Now they had cash in the bank and the land was stocked to its capacity. As the money mounted Tom would regularly repeat a phrase which he had coined the day he discovered he was out of the red. 'Thrift won't lose,' he would say, 'because thrift can't lose'. The logic of his composition appealed more and more to him as the years went by.

He was well aware that his neighbours and those who knew him further afield criticised him constantly for what he considered to be one of the great virtues. His parsimony had become something of a local joke. Those who conducted church gate collections for various charities would nudge each other when Tom Cutler approached. He never subscribed no matter how worthy the cause. As soon as he had passed the collection tables he would permit himself the faintest of smiles. He smiled purely and simply because he still had his money. That, to Tom Cutler, was a genuine cause for mirth. He really relished such incidents. They were the only luxuries in which he indulged.

His son John, on the other hand, was known as a decent type. He hadn't much, his neighbours said, but by God that much was yours if you wanted it.

'He didn't bring it from his father,' Mick Kelly would say, "tis from the grandfather he brought it, his father's father. Now there was your decent man. Give you the shirt off his back he would.'

Inevitably these assessments of his son would be relayed back one way or another to Tom. They occasioned him many a smile. So John was like his grandfather, was he, the same grandfather who drank himself to death and mortgaged the farm up to the hilt, the same grandfather who couldn't call on a shilling to bury the wife who died prematurely from shame. Tom had been forced to surrender the few pounds he had saved through his teens to buy a cheap coffin and have High Mass said for his mother. It had been a bitter lesson. His father had shamed him into putting up the money. He resolved immediately after his mother's funeral that his financial standing would never be revealed to anybody again, not even to his wife. Oh she knew he had money and she might guess rightly that it was a tidy bit but in this respect she would be close-mouthed because no matter how much she might crave after a commodity her need for security outweighed all else. From the start she had wanted him to part with his money. First the curtains hadn't been good enough, then the furniture, then the wallpaper and inevitably the house itself. He had always heard her out patiently. He would put her off with promises but as the years passed and he began to accumulate a little money he was able to boast that his frugality was paying off. In time she began to see that he had been right.

'Wouldn't we be in a nice way now,' he often told her, 'if I had given in.'

He had another son Willie, a subcontractor in England. A thrifty man was Willie. On the day of his departure Tom had handed him his fare and a ten pound note.

'If you have any sense,' he warned him, 'you'll not break that note needlessly. Put it aside and soon you'll have another to keep it company.'

And how much had Willie today? Willie had plenty because he had listened. More important nobody but Willie himself knew how much Willie had. That was the trouble about possessing money. You might spend years saving it while your very own kin had no thought but to squander it while you'd say Jack Robinson.

John Cutler's attitude towards his parents changed dramatically after the confrontation. It had been his wont each night upon returning home from the pub to impart the latest gossip going the rounds and to give an account of the activities of the pub's patrons if such activities warranted it. His parents looked forward to this nightly report, especially his father although he never commented, whatever the content. He enjoyed it all the more because it cost nothing. They would have retired before his arrival but the bedroom door would be partly open in expectation.

Now there was no communication between them. Tom and Minnie were not unduly worried. He had sulked before but had come out of it after a few days. This time it was to be different. Weeks went by and then months until Tom closed the bedroom door to show that he didn't care. Around this time John started to grow careless about his appearance. Frequently too he came home drunk from the pub. Some mornings he was unable to rise for the milking. Minnie grew worried when she over-heard him talking in his room. She relayed the news to Tom who put it down to drink.

'Wasn't I the wise man.' he told her, 'to hold on to what I had. Wouldn't we be in a nice way now depending on a drunkard.'

The rift became worse when John demanded an increase in wages.

'What do you want it for?' his father asked curtly.

'I need it to keep pace,' John answered patiently.

'To keep pace with what, the price of drink is it?'

'There's more than drink gone up and well you know it. I need a new suit and a few shirts. My best shoes are beyond repair.'

'Wait till the fall of the year,' had been Tom Cutler's response. 'I'll know better where I stand.'

'And the rise?'

'I don't see what you need a rise for unless 'tis drink.'

The old man had gone to the bedroom and locked himself in to avoid further argument. In despair John went straight to the pub where he stayed till midnight. When he came home he tried to open the bedroom door but it was still locked. They could hear him in the kitchen talking to himself. Neither said

70

a word for a long while. Finally Minnie broke the silence. She spoke in a whisper not wishing her voice to carry.

'Would it not be better to relent a little?' she suggested.

'No.' Tom's reply was emphatic.

'But he's acting so queerly.'

'You want me to give in to a madman is that it?'

'No, no, that's not it at all. All I want is for you to make a concession.'

'I'll make no concession to drink woman and that is that. Now go to sleep.'

Minnie Cutler sighed. After a while she spoke for the last time before falling asleep.

'Who's to say but you're right,' she said.

The following evening Mick Kelly the postman called. He came in his Sunday clothes. The old folk welcomed him. There was no sign of John.

'Sit down, sit down.' Tom Cutler pulled a chair from under the table and placed it near the fire.

'And how's herself?' Minnie Cutler asked.

'Never better missus thank you,' Mick Kelly replied cheerfully.

In any other house in the neighbourhood he would have been royally received. The whiskey bottle would have appeared. The kettle would have been put down to boil. Minnie who was never embarrassed by similar situations fumbled for words on this occasion but could find none. Mick Kelly was a good neighbour. For once she would have liked to offer him something. Her husband read her thoughts.

'I daresay you've had your supper Mick,' he said with forced joviality.

'Just after rising from the table,' came the answer.

71

'You're welcome to eat, you know that,' Minnie spoke half-heartedly.

'Oh I know that missus,' came the reassuring reply, 'I know that well.'

He made it sound convincing to put Minnie at her ease. He could not recall ever having received as much as a mouthful of tea at Cutler's. Neither could anybody else. Even the beggars of the roadway gave the place a wide berth. Some said there were barely visible scratches on the gate piers down by the main road, the secret sign language of the tinker folk: 'Pass by' the scratches said or so it was believed.

For an hour or more the three spoke of weather, crops and cattle, then of the neighbours and lastly of the great wide world. The ancient Stanley range had grown cold for want of fuelling. There were a few embers buried in the ashes but to stoke the firebox would be to despatch its entire contents into the ashpan beneath. Mick Kelly knew that it would be unthinkable for the Cutlers to replenish the fire so late in the evening.

'Well,' said he and he rose from his chair, 'I'll have to be going but before I do I had better bring out what brought me.' He cleared his throat and rubbed his large hands together, this to intimate that his mission was a delicate one.

'I've come about John,' he said. 'You may tell me it's none of my business but I have known the three of you all my life and I feel I have earned the right to bring this matter to your notice.' Here he paused waiting for word to proceed.

'What is it about John?' Tom Cutler asked.

'He's not himself these days,' Mick Kelly answered. 'He's drinking too much and he's in debt poor fellow. It's not a lot, a few pounds here and there. He owes myself a tenner but that's not why I'm here and I'd gladly forget it if I thought it would help the man.'

'Let him stop drinking and he'll soon have his debts paid,' Tom cut in.

'I'm afraid,' Mick Kelly spoke ruefully, 'most of the drink comes from people who are sorry for him.'

'He's turned into a bum then has he?'

'No. That isn't so at all. Most people will throw a drink a fellow's way if they think he has a problem. It's their way of sympathising.'

'What do you want me to do?'

'Rise his wage for a start. Give the poor fellow a few hundred to pay his debts. That's all. I promise you won't know the man after.'

'I'll tell you something now Mick Kelly and I'll tell you no more.' Tom Cutler rose and faced him. He moistened his thin lips before he spoke. 'When I took over here there was a crippling debt. I was advised to sell but I stuck it out whatever. It took the best years of my life to pay back the money my father squandered. It was a terrible burden for a young man and now when I'm old you want me to pay my son's debts as well. Is that to be the story of my life, to pay back the debts of two drunkards, my father and my son?'

'I can't counsel you further Tom,' Mick Kelly said quietly. 'I can only tell you that all is not well with your son.'

'It's not my doing Mick.'

'I didn't say it was Tom. The poor fellow is demented and what harm but he could have enough if he wanted but he's too bloody honest.'

'I don't follow you,' Tom Cutler frowned.

'He could be selling the odd bag of corn behind your back

73

and he could be transferring a gallon or two of milk to a crony. There's a lot doing it and getting away with it but not John Cutler. He could be lifting the occasional bag of spuds.'

Tom Cutler stamped the concrete floor with his right foot. 'He could in his eye,' he whipped back. 'If there was a grain of corn taken, or a single spud or a solitary pint of milk I'd know about it. He knows that. You know that and I know that and that's the reason he hasn't lifted anything so far. His first time would be his last time. I have another son, remember, a man who wouldn't be long answering my call if I sent for him.'

'I beg of you Tom not to renege on John.' Mick Kelly's appeal was fervent.

'I never reneged on him. He had cattle of his own remember. He drank the proceeds every time.'

'And I tell you he drank no more than anybody else.' Mick Kelly stuck to his purpose.

'I'm tired, Mick.' Tom Cutler returned to his chair.

He was making it clear that as far as he was concerned the discussion was closed. Mick Kelly looked from husband to wife. For a moment he considered making a final appeal but thought better of it. The eyes of both were now focused on the ashpan of the Stanley. They leaned forward on their chairs the better to gaze upon it. As well as dismissing him the pose also suggested a show of solidarity.

'Goodnight,' Mick Kelly threw back as he opened the kitchen door.

'Goodnight Mick,' they spoke in unison without averting their heads. Mick felt as if he had closed the door on a tomb. He hurried home to his wife. He had promised to tell her how he fared before going to the pub.

As soon as the fall of the year had established itself John

Cutler laid it on the line for the old man.

'I need decking out from head to toes,' he said, 'and it cannot be put off any longer. You will also double the money you are paying me now. Nothing less will do. Any farmer in the neighbourhood would do better by me.'

'Let me think about that one for a while,' Tom Cutler had told him. 'The fall isn't full out yet you know.'

It was the way the old man had said it that nettled John. It was as though he had made some outrageously childish claim and had not been taken seriously, had been humorously rebuffed. Was his father playing for time and if so why? The old fellow had been acting too independently of late, not caring whether John rose or slept it out in the mornings, whistling to himself and walking off whenever John grumbled about his lot. It was a totally new and inexplicable phase in their relationship. Had the old man something up his sleeve? John grew moodier as the autumn drew to a close. He was no longer asked to go to the village for farm or household necessities. He suspected he was being subtly isolated. Whenever he entered the kitchen they busied themselves ostentatiously with needless chores or if they were engaged in conversation it was immediately terminated when he put in an appearance. It was as though his father wished him to know that he had better tread warily, that there might be more strings to his bow than were apparent. There could only be one answer. They had contacted Willie with a view to bringing him home but how to be sure, how to make certain? Mick Kelly would know.

'It's a question I am not at liberty to answer,' Mick Kelly told him firmly when John Cutler demanded to know if there had been any exchange of letters between his father and Willie.

'Then there is!' John banged his pint glass triumphantly on

the bar counter.

'No,' Mick assured him, 'there isn't. Take my word for it. You have nothing to worry about from that quarter, at least as far as I know.'

John shook his head glumly. 'He has some ace in the hole,' he said, 'it has to be Willie.'

The Cutlers did not possess a motor car. The only concession Tom Cutler had made to modernisation was to invest in a second-hand tractor and he did this reluctantly. Until the arrival of the tractor he depended on a pair of horses. He greatly deprecated the disposal of these but compensated himself with the purchase of a pony. He refused to buy a motor car. He had a light cart made for the pony and used it to convey himself and Minnie to Mass, for occasional trips to the village and for work in the bog during the turf harvesting. The tractor with a trailer attached was used chiefly for conveying the milk to the village creamery and for general farm work although John used it regularly to get to and from the pub.

As they breakfasted one morning towards the end of September the old man addressed his wife.

'As soon as you've finished the washing-up,' he informed her, 'I'll tackle the pony for you. There's a few items to be got from the village.'

Minnie nodded obediently.

'You'll bring the usual groceries, a quarter pound of three inch nails and eight yards of rope. 'Tis time the turf was drawn out. The laths on the rail need securing and a new reins will be wanted.'

Again Minnie nodded dutifully. 'Will that be all?' she asked.

'That will be all,' Tom Cutler said.

'Bring a handful of fags as well will you?' John added.

The old couple exchanged looks but no comment was forthcoming. Tom arose and went towards the door. Before going out he turned. 'You will bring back the items I ordered,' he said, 'and no more.' Hands in pockets he went whistling into the sunlight.

Without a word John rose and followed. His mother would have restrained him but he was gone before she could speak. What she wanted to tell him was that she would bring a few packets of cigarettes unknown to his father but the words just wouldn't come out. She had been frightened by the look on John's face as he left. At first she feared that he would waylay his father and have it out with him but no, he had gone straight to the tractor, started it and driven off. Mick Kelly's words came back to her. 'I can't counsel you further,' he had said. 'I can only tell you that all is not well with your son.'

From force of habit she refused to ponder on the problem, concentrating instead on the trip to the village. She sensed, however, that events were coming to a head. Her intuition told her that something would have to be done if a calamity were to be avoided. There was no point in bringing the matter up with her husband. She had tried repeatedly since Mick Kelly's visit but he had smothered every effort at the outset. She resorted to the only means of succour remaining to her. Rummaging in her apron pocket she withdrew her Rosary beads and silently began the long count of Hail Marys. She would pray the whole way to and from the village and she would light candles in the parish church. The thought consoled her. The peace and beauty of the candle altar would be a tonic in itself, the very thing to bring her out of herself. She was unaccustomed to such treats. As she led the pony towards the roadway there was a lightness in her step that she hadn't experienced for months. In the village she saw a tractor which looked like John's outside one of the public houses but her new found elation was such that she felt able to ignore the implications involved. In the church she would find refuge from all embarrassments. There was no doubt in her mind about that and was not this as it should be? Was it not her entitlement?

Mick Kelly dismounted from his motor cycle at the entrance to the Cutler farm. He didn't have a letter but he had resolved to face up to Tom Cutler a second time. The day before he had encountered Minnie on her way from the village but she had not reined up to talk. Neither had she returned his salute. He had noticed the beads entwined about her fingers. He had remounted then and gone about his business. He had planned a new approach for this second appeal. This time he would draw Minnie into the thick of things whether she wished it or not. He believed that deep down she sympathised with John and he would be depending on this. It would be to his advantage if she were alone when he arrived but failing that he would involve her anyway. As he neared the house he sensed there was something wrong, something disproportionate. There was a new and terrible dimension to the area left of the house where the last leaves on a stand of ash trees whispered in the morning wind. There was an ominous addition to the familiar landscape and yet, though he was curious, he could not bring himself to look. This, however, could be that he already knew the awful nature of the intrusion. Slowly he forced his eyes to the left, eyes that started to fill with terror the moment he decided to confirm his worst fears. What he saw before him was the ultimate in physical distortion. The body of John Cutler hung from a stout branch extending from one of the ash trees. Around his neck was the shining new rope his mother had purchased in the village the day before. He was barefoot. His shoes had fallen to the ground. They lay directly beneath his feet. Mick Kelly made the sign of the cross and threw the cycle to one side. His next reaction was to pound the kitchen door. Instead he drew a deep breath and knocked gently. The door was opened at once by Tom Cutler.

'I have bad news.' Mick Kelly bent his head to avoid the rheumy eyes. Tom Cutler made his task easy.

'I know,' he said, 'I was just going for help.'

He had, he explained, been changing into a fresh shirt. His shortcoat lay in readiness on the table. Minnie sat soundlessly by the Stanley, her beads clutched in her hands, her body rocking forward and backwards on the chair. All the time her lips moved in prayer.

'Will you take him down?' Tom Cutler asked.

'Yes, of course,' Mick answered, surprised by the old man's matter-of-factness. Despite the shock which he must have undergone he seemed to be his everyday self.

'You'll need a ladder,' Tom Cutler said.

'And a knife,' Mick enjoined.

'What do you want with a knife?' Tom asked.

'To cut the rope,' Mick responded.

'A saw is what you want,' Tom reminded him. 'A saw to cut the branch.'

Mick listened with growing wonder as the old man explained. 'A branch can be had for nothing,' he said, 'a rope costs money. Besides 'tis wanted for a reins.'

Buttoning his shortcoat he led the way to a small outhouse. He emerged with a short ladder which he handed to Mick. He re-entered the house and emerged with a rusty saw.

He motioned a bemused Mick Kelly to follow him towards the ash grove. Overhead the dry leaves flickered around his dead son. Some fell to the ground to join the others already rotting there.

7
DOUSIE O'DEA

If you were to ask anybody in the parish of Tanvally about Dousie O'Dea the answer would always be the same. She had no equal in the county when it came to the doing up of corpses. As she grew older she grew selective and practised her art on rare occasions only. Then there came an unhappy day when she announced that she was retiring altogether. Thereafter nothing could persuade her to continue. She declined even to indulge deathbed wishes.

It was in the little things that Dousie excelled. Where a wart dominated a certain area of the face when life throbbed in that face's temples there would be no sign in death that a wart ever existed. Hair that in life seemed lank and incapable of curling assumed, under Dousie's coiffeusage, a transfiguration so beauteous that seasoned corpse-viewers could only gasp upon beholding it. She had a special way with wrinkles. As she kneaded the ancient skin of pensioners these would vanish mysteriously one by one until the texture of the skin on the face of the subject assumed a girlish smoothness. Unsightly pimples were transformed into fetching beauty spots while minor distortions of the neck and ears were so skilfully adapted that they never failed to compliment the visage from which they once detracted.

Once and once only was her handiwork submitted for professional criticism. The cadaver in question was that of one Baldy Mullane, an aged agricultural labourer who suddenly made his farewell to this life while transplanting onions in a plot at the rear of his cottage. Dousie was called upon to ready him for his trip to the next world. This she did without fuss or delay. That night at Baldy Mullane's wake there was porter in abundance. Two half tierces were on tap. Wine and whiskey flowed freely. It had been Baldy's lifelong ambition to be waked decently. At the height of the mourning when the wake-room was crammed with sympathisers it was announced that an American holiday-maker by the name of Louis Blep had arrived for the dual purpose of paying his respects and inspecting the corpse. Blep was a small, fat, loquacious individual whose mother had been born and reared in Tanvally but was forced to emigrate to the United States in order to find employment. In Chicago she married a successful mortician of German extraction. His name was Ernst Blep. Louis was the sole outcome of the union. Ever since his Confirmation when his mother had first brought him on holiday to her parents' home in Tanvally Louis had paid regular visits to the maternal homestead. His mother and grandparents were long since dead but there was no scarcity of relations. He would spend a few days with each until his three weeks' holiday expired. Even if he had never heard of Dousie O'Dea's skills as an amateur mortician his presence would have been expected at the wake-house anyway.

He was greeted on arrival by Baldy Mullane's daughter, Bessie. A brimming glass of whiskey was thrust into his hand. He swallowed it neat at one go. This was the custom. He would be presented with a second glass as soon as he regained his breath after the first. This would be drunk at a more leisurely rate while he sympathised with the relations. As soon as he moved towards the wake-room door the occupants of the kitchen pressed forward. There were many who wanted to hear him confirm what they had long believed, that Dousie O'Dea was without peer when it came to the doing-up of corpses while others, a minority, hoped only that the visit would be a come-uppance for Dousie. Such is the price of fame and indeed in Tanvally as in other places there are always people who are incapable of saying a good word about anybody.

Preparatory to his entry Louis Blep handed his empty glass to Bessie Mullane. It would hardly have been in keeping with the occasion had he taken it into the wake-room. Handing it to Bessie was his guarantee that it would be filled upon his return to the kitchen. Louis hesitated for a moment at the wake-room door. He had already resolved to be uncritical of Dousie's efforts. Neither would he over-praise. A pleasant smile and a gentle nod of approval should keep everybody happy. He was quite unprepared for the eye-catching artistry which confronted him from the death bed. Baldy Mullane did not look a day over forty. His head glinted under the light of the sacred candles which stood in their pewter sticks at either side of the bed. The serenity of sanctity shone from his flawless face. If the expression thereon could have been translated into words it would have read: 'Gone straight to heaven. Signed Baldy Mullane'.

Louis knelt on one knee and whispered a hasty Lord's Prayer for the soul of the deceased. A number of sombrely dressed, elderly women sat on sugawn chairs at the other side of the bed. Their trained eyes missed nothing. If Louis Blep's inscrutable features were to register the most insignificant of changes it would be recorded at once and its character accurately interpreted. From time to time these frosty-faced fossils exchanged whispers, winks and nudges which spelt approval or disapproval of certain mourners. Otherwise they maintained a stony silence which helped immediately to chasten exuberant or drunken visitors. In fairness to them they helped to preserve the solemnity of the proceedings. Louis Blep rose and blessed himself, nodded respectfully in the direction of the vigilant elders and vacated the wake-room. A crowd gathered round him. He took momentary refuge in the full glass which Bessie Mullane handed him.

'Well?' A self-appointed spokesman for the group posed the question.

'I seen mugs in my time,' Louis Blep, having carefully considered the question, spoke from his heart, 'but I ain't never seen no mug like that in there. The guy's positively beautiful. This dame, what's her name?'

'Dousie O'Dea,' everybody chorused.

'She's a natcheral. If she was in the States with a talent like that she'd be a millionaire in no time.'

This put the seal on Dousie O'Dea's already prestigious reputation. Word of Louis Blep's commendation spread far and wide. From that night forth it was considered sacrilegious when unwittingly some innocent spoke disparagingly of Dousie. Her reputation was secure. That was why her retirement came as such a blow to those who had hoped for her ministrations at the end. Years passed but despite constant appeals she steadfastly refused to come out of retirement. As a result it greatly added to the respectability of a family if they could boast that one of their members had been done up by Dousie O'Dea. It was almost like owning a Stradivarius. It carried with it more esteem than a marble headstone or a Celtic Cross and it wasn't that Dousie had lost her touch or that age had blunted her skill.

In her heart of hearts she knew that all her efforts, excellent and all as they were, had a sameness, an unchangeable texture, a sort of futile duplication. The cold truth was that no single one stood out above any other. No one would deny that they were all masterpieces and could not be bettered but was this enough? Should not there be one effort which crowned all the others? It was a niggling question and the older she got the more it vexed her. Hard as she tried she could not recall a particular corpse more pleasing to her than all the others. From her backward vantage point she had no way of knowing that the true artist can never be fully satisfied.

In time others came to take her place. She frequently viewed the end-products of her imitators. She had no choice. When neighbours died condolences had to be offered. This meant kneeling by the deathbed for as long as it took to intone a decade of the Rosary. She would have to be blind not to notice the bed's occupant. Always upon rising she would pass the same comment: 'A handsome corpse God bless her', or if it was a man: 'A noble corpse God bless him'. She was conceding nothing. Everybody else said exactly the same thing. It was part of the ritual of all wake-house visits. Sometimes when her imitators excelled themselves the grim-faced custodians of the wake-room would alert themselves for Dousie's reaction. None save the customary comment was ever forthcoming. Then on a hail-ridden, windy night in mid-January Dousie O'Dea had unexpected visitors. Her husband Jack it was who answered the timid knocking on the door. Jack and Dousie had not been blessed with issue. For all that they were well content with themselves and had no great wish for company other than their own.

'Who's out?' Jack O'Dea called.

''Tis only us,' came the response from outside.

'Yes,' said Jack O'Dea, 'but who is us?'

'Us is Thade and Donal Fizzell.'

Jack recognised Thade Fizzell's booming voice.

'I declare to God!' Dousie spoke from her corner of the hearth, 'there is nothing so sure as that their sister Jule is dead.'

In the doorway the brothers shook the hailstones from their caps and shoulders.

'God bless all here.' They spoke in unison.

'Take off the coats and drive on up to the fire,' Dousie welcomed them as she rose to take their coats.

''Tis unmerciful weather entirely,' Thade Fizzell spoke to no one in particular.

'A coarse brush I wouldn't put out this night,' Donal, the smaller and younger of the pair spoke in support. When all were seated round the fire Dousie took a bottle and glasses from a well-concealed compartment high in the hearth wall. The bottle contained poitcheen. She poured until the brothers protested and then poured an extra dollop in case the protests were token. The brothers were well into their second glasses before conversation began in earnest. It touched first upon the vagaries of the winter weather, then upon the quality of fodder and potatoes until it centred upon the true purpose of the visit. The externals, however, had to be observed regardless of the importance of the news. These outward flourishes helped to emphasise the main item which in this case happened to be, as Dousie had predicted, the recent demise of Jule Fizzell. The brothers were both in their early seventies which meant that Jule who was the oldest of the family could well be eighty years of age.

'Did she go quick the poor soul?' Dousie enquired after

her death had been announced.

'Like that,' Thade Fizzell replied and flicked his fingers to indicate the speed of her departure.

'Darning socks she was in front of the fire when the needle tinkled on the hearthstone and the sock fell from her hand.'

'May God grant a silver bed in heaven,' the aspiration came from Jack O'Dea.

'You know, of course,' Thade Fizzell cut short the celestial entreaties, 'she was anything but a handsome woman.'

The O'Deas nodded sympathetically and waited.

'In fact,' Thade continued, 'you'd be hard put to find uglier.'

'She was,' Donal Fizzell subscribed, 'the plainest creature I ever came across. I must say in truth, although she was my very own sister, that I used to keep a look-out in my travels for plainer but I looked in vain. Our Jule beat all I ever saw. That woman used to frighten the children on their way home from school. Even the crows avoided our haggard when she cocked her head in the air.'

When Donal finished Thade resumed.

'At dances long ago men used to talk sideways at the poor creature so as to avoid looking at her direct. In the end she gave up going to dances and contented herself by her own hearth. Matchmakers came with accounts of likely men but one look was enough for them. What harm but she was as kind-hearted a soul as ever drew breath. There was a great heart cooped inside her breast and I never heard her cast a hard word on any creature living or dead.'

Thade Fizzell noted the tears that trickled down Dousie O'Dea's face. He nudged his brother. Donal maintained the advocacy. 'That dear soul,' he continued, 'wanted nothing only to see others happy but she did make one request. Every so often she would say, "There is something you boys must do for me". We never had to ask what it was. We knew it well enough from listening day in, day out. "When I'm stretched on my deathbed you'll bring Dousie O'Dea to do me up". It wasn't for the Pope of Rome she asked nor cardinals with their red hats. All she wanted was to be done up by Dousie O'Dea.'

A long, awkward silence followed. It was Jack O'Dea who broke it.

'Boys,' he said, 'Dousie is greatly honoured by all you say but what you ask is impossible.'

'Then let her tell us herself,' Thade Fizzell insisted. 'We are, at the very least, entitled to that.'

'It is as Jack says,' Dousie spoke with finality.

'With a face like Jule's,' Donal Fizzell said sadly, 'there is no hope she'll face for heaven. She'd be too ashamed. She'll most likely linger at the gate forever. I daresay it was too much to ask in the first place for there is no power on earth could transform our eyesore of a sister into a presentable corpse. It just cannot be done.'

'I did not say it could not be done,' Dousie cut in pertly.

'Then you'll do it?' New hope radiated from Thade's amiable face.

'I didn't say that either,' Dousie reminded him, 'but in view of all you have said and taking into account what your poor sister suffered in this world because of her looks I'll do her up for you but it will be the last time these hands will ever decorate the dead.'

The brothers Fizzell could scarcely contain their delight. Old as they were they danced a jig on the flagstone of the hearth but stopped suddenly when Jack O'Dea reminded them that a sister of theirs lay dead. Dousie took immediate charge of the situation as soon s the brothers' rejoicing had fully subsided.

'Jack,' she said, 'you go straightaway and tackle the cob. You boys go on home and make arrangements for the wake. I'm going to the room for to gather my accoutrements.'

At Fizzell's Dousie worked alone and in silence. She saw to it that the wake-room door was bolted from the inside. She had long determined that her craft, for what it was worth, would go to the grave with her. It had often been suggested that she adopt an apprenctice or at least school some of the corpse-dressers who appeared after her retirement in the basics of the business. She had turned a deaf ear to such entreaties. She was well aware that any disclosure on her part would quickly erode the reverence in which she was held. Anyway it was her strongly held contention that corpse-dressers, like poets, were born, not made. Jule Fizzell proved to be the most difficult subject she had ever encountered. Luckily she had lost none of her old skill. Neither did her long lay-off impede the work in any way. An hour passed and then another. A voice from the kitchen asked if everything was all right. She replied in the affirmative and asked that there be no more such queries. She needed every last iota of her concentration for the job in hand. Indeed there were times when she despaired of effecting any change whatsoever, so complex and craggy were the features under hands. Perspiration trickled down her face as the night wore on. Yet she persevered until slowly but surely a masterpiece began to take shape. She became a trifle excited as she realised that this might well be the central gem in the wide brooch of her art. In the end, after nearly three hours of sustained effort, she had accomplished the impossible. She sat triumphantly on the bedside of her subject and for the first time in her life savoured the heady brew of total artistic satisfaction.

'That's not our sister,' were the first words uttered by Donal Fizzell.

Thade simply stood transfixed. After a while he spoke. 'It's our sister all right,' he said, 'and it's what she might have been like if God had ordained it so.'

Jack O'Dea was aware from the moment his eyes met those of his wife that something extraordinary had taken place. When he surveyed the corpse he felt some of the ecstasy that she had felt. Before him on the bed lay one of the most beautiful women he had ever seen. The face that was once a travesty was now angelic, its sharp contours magically soften- ed by the artistry of his wife. The Fizzell brothers had seated themselves on chairs, their unbelieving eyes firmly fixed on the ravishing creature on the deathbed. Now and then they would shake their heads or exchange mystified looks but no words came. The fact was that there were no words which would do proper justice to Dousie's creation. If there was a word that might be fittingly applied that word was alive for, in truth, Jule Fizzell had never looked more alive. In life men had looked the other way. In death they would look at Jule Fizzell a second time and remember her haunting beauty long after she had been claimed by the clay. After what seemed like hours the brothers stirred themselves from the trance which had mesmerised them. There was the wake to think of. The undertaker would have to be approached. Drink would need to be transported from the village. Victuals in plenty would have to be purchased, relative notified and the hundred and one other items attended to, which all went into the making of a successful wake.

In the parish of Tanvally there are nights which are remembered above all others. There was, for instance, the night of the big wind and the night of Horan's last wren-dance. Of like calibre was the night of Jule Fizzell's wake. The mourners came from far and wide. Single, in pairs and in droves they came to view the Fizzell phenomenon. Those who had known her personally were awe-struck by the transformation. Those who came merely out of curiosity were lavish in their praise. None could recall a corpse possessed of so much charm and vivacity. The wake was a success from the outset. Instead of proving to be an embarrassment, as the brothers had feared, their departed sister had brought them honour and glory. They swaggered from kitchen to wake-room accepting sympathy and homage. Midway through the wake the drink supply ran dangerously low. A courier was quickly despatched to the village where the original order was repeated. It was delivered instantly. The publican in question was requested to be on hand should further supplies be needed. Thade and Donal Fizzell were determined to play their part in making the night a memorable one. Neighbours were commissioned to ensure that no glass remained empty for long. Pots of tea and plates of edibles were in constant circulation. By midnight the house was packed to suffocation. The sole topic of conversation was the corpse. She was showered with superlatives. Hardened reprobates whose previous wake room contributions rarely exceeded a single, mumbled prayer spent long periods on their knees, their eyes affixed to the deathbed whereon lay the loveliest creature they had ever beheld. There were many who revisited the wake-room several times. These consisted mainly of those who could not at first believe their eyes.

At one o'clock in the morning the drift homewards began. By four the house was deserted save for Thade and Donal Fizzell and a few cronies who elected to keep them company until daybreak. Having consumed their fill of drink the entire party lapsed into a drunken sleep around the fire. When they wakened in the morning the corpse had vanished. They looked under the bed but all they found there was a venerable chamber pot which had seen better days. They looked in the other rooms but found no trace of the missing cadaver.

While they had slept a strange thing had happened. In the Tanvally uplands, on a small isolated farm there resided a rough and ready sort of a fellow known far and wide as the Cowboy Cooney. No one knew for sure what his exact age might be. It was certain, however, that he was no chicken. He lived completely alone with neither chick nor child, wife nor parent. His only visitors were poitcheen dealers who came at monthly intervals to purchase his regular output of the precious brew. If, on rare occasions, other callers appeared on the narrow roadway which led to his house he made himself scarce in the hills and did not return till they had departed. From early afternoon he had been aware that something of importance had happened in the valley. As night came down and the lights of a hundred transports twinkled on the main road several miles below he grew alarmed.

'What can it mean?' he asked himself. Had there been an invasion of some kind? Had some unprecedented disaster struck the valley? He withdrew a poitcheen bottle from underneath the thatch and positioned himself on the pier of a gate the better to view the goings-on in the valley. Lights in their hundreds came and went. With over half the contents of the bottle safely tucked away the Cowboy decided that the activities down below merited his personal attention. He decided to bring the bottle with him for company. By the time he reached the Fizzel farmhouse which had seemed to him to be the nub of the bustle he saw only the sleeping figures by the fire. Cautiously he entered and surveyed the scene. On the table standing out from several empty contemporaries was a full bottle of whiskey. Since he had long since emptied his own bottle he put this welcome find to his head and downed at least two glasses in one long, single swallow. It was quite palatable although a lightweight concoction compared to his own home-made draughts. He sensed rather than saw that the cause of all the earlier comings and goings was to be found in the room so romantically flooded by flickering candle-light. He was not prepared for the sight which met his eyes. He stood with his mouth open for several moments utterly overcome by the radiant loveliness of the smiling lady who occupied the bed. It was this very smile which gave him the courage to advance a step or two. The Cowboy Cooney up until this moment had always been the very soul of shyness. This was no longer the case. The smile on the face of this wonderful woman on whom he had never before laid eyes had given him poise and confidence. He could see that she wished him to sit on the side of the bed. This he did and at once launched into the story of his life. He wept throughout the tragic aspects and the smile on her face seemed to change to one of sympathy. Emboldened by her obvious fondness for him he took her hand not noticing the coldness.

'Will you marry me?' he asked.

At this she merely smiled but he could see that it was a smile of consent. What a placid, sensitive, modest creature she was.

'Then you'll be mine?' he asked. Again the affirming smile.

'There is no need to speak,' he told her, 'your smile has spoken for you.'

Gently he lifted her into his arms and staggered into the kitchen where he addressed the sleeping inmates.

'I am taking this woman to be my lawful wedded wife,' he announced. 'If any man here has anything to say let him speak now or forever hold his peace.'

He waited for a reply and was rewarded with an assortment of drunken snores which he took to mean approval. Triumphantly he blundered into the night. Next morning they were discovered by a group of school-children. Jule Fizzell was cradled in the arms of Cowboy Cooney. The serene smile on his face was matched only by that on the face of the corpse. He snored blissfully. She made no sound at all.

When, later in the day, the news was relayed to Dousie O'Dea she smiled to herself. She had reached the final pinnacle. Her life's work was complete. For one man she had brought the dead to life. For this, in itself, she would be remembered beyond the grave.

8
THE WOMAN WHO HATED CHRISTMAS

Polly Baun did not hate Christmas as some of her more un-charitable neighbours would have people believe. She merely disliked it. She was once accused by a local drunkard of trying to call a halt to Christmas. She was on her way out of church at the time and the drunkard, who celebrated his own form of mass by criticising the sermon while he leaned against the outside wall of the church, was seen to push her on the back as she passed the spot where he leaned. As a result Polly Baun fell forward and was rendered immobile for a week. She told her husband that she had slipped on a banana skin because he was a short-tempered chap. However, he found out from another drunkard who frequented the same tavern that Polly had been pushed. When he confronted her with his findings she reluctantly conceded that the second drunkard had been telling the truth.

'You won't do anything rash!' she beseeched him.

'I won't do anything rash,' Shaun Baun promised, 'but you will have to agree that this man's energies must be directed in another direction. I mean we can't have him pushing women to the ground because he disagrees with their views. I mean,' he continued in what he believed to be a reasonable tone, 'if this sort of thing is allowed to go on unchecked no woman will be safe.'

'It doesn't worry me in the least,' Polly Baun assured him.

'That may be,' he returned, 'but the fact of the matter is

that no woman deserves to be pushed to the ground.'

Polly Baun decided that the time had come to terminate the conversation. It was leading nowhere to begin with and she was afraid she might say something that would infuriate her husband. He flew off the handle easily but generally he would return to his normal state of complacency after a few brief moments.

As Christmas approached, the street shed its everyday look and donned the finery of the season. Polly Baun made one of her few concessions to Christmas by buying a goose. It was a young goose, small but plump and, most importantly, purchased from an accredited goose breeder. It would suit the two of them nicely. There were no children and there would be no Christmas guests and Polly who was of a thrifty disposition judged that there would also be enough for Saint Stephen's Day. She did not need to be thrifty. The hat shop behind which they lived did a tidy business. The tiny kitchen at the rear of the shop served a threefold purpose all told. As well as being a kitchen it was also a dining area and sitting-room. They might have added on but Polly failed to see the need for this. She was content with what she had and she felt that one of the chief problems with the world was that people did not know when they were well off.

'They should be on their knees all day thanking God,' she would tell her husband when he brought news of malcontents who lived only to whine.

Shaun Baun sought out and isolated his wife's attacker one wet night a week before Christmas. The scoundrel was in the habit of taking a turn around the town before retiring to the pub for the evening. Shaun Baun did not want to take advantage of him while he might be in his cups and besides he wanted him sober enough to fully understand the enormity of his transgressions.

'You sir!' Shaun Baun addressed his victim in a secluded side street, 'are not a gentleman and neither are you any other kind of man. You knocked my wife to the ground and did not bother to go to her assistance.'

'I was drunk,' came back the reply.

'Being drunk is not sufficient justification for pushing a woman to the ground.'

'I was told,' the drunkard's voice was filled with fear, 'that she hates Christmas.'

'That is not sufficient justification either,' Shaun insisted. The drunkard began to back off as Shaun assumed a fighting pose.

'Before I clobber you,' Shaun Baun announced grimly, 'I feel obliged to correct a mistaken impression you have. My wife does not hate Christmas as you would infer. My wife simply discourages Christmas which is an entirely different matter.' So saying Shaun feinted, snorted, shuffled and finally landed a nose-breaking blow which saw the drunkard fall to the ground with a cry of pain. At once Shaun extended a helping hand and brought him to his feet where he assured him that full retribution had been extracted and that the matter was closed.

'However,' Shaun drew himself up to his full height which was five feet one and a half inches, 'if you so much as look at my wife from this day forth I will break both your legs.'

The drunkard nodded his head eagerly, earnestly indicating that he had taken the warning to heart. He would, in the course of time, intimidate other women but he would never thereafter have anything to do with Polly. For her part Polly would never know that an assault had taken place. Shaun would never tell her. She would only disapprove. She would continue to discourage Christmas as was her wont and, with this in mind, she decided to remove all the chairs from the kitchen and place them in the backyard until Christmas had run its course. If, she quite rightly deduced, there were no chairs for those who made Christmas visits they would not be able to sit down and, therefore, their visits would be of short duration.

On the day before Christmas Eve the hat shop was busy. Occasionally when a purchase was made the wearer would first defer to Polly's judgement. This, of course, necessitated a trip to the kitchen. The practice had been in existence for years. Countrymen in particular and confirmed bachelors would make the short trip to the kitchen to have their hats or caps inspected. On getting the nod from Polly Baun they would return to the shop and pay Shaun for their purchases. Sometimes Polly would disapprove of the colour and other times she would disapprove of the shape. There were times when she would shake her head because of the hat's size or because of its rim or because of its crown. Shaun Baun's trade flourished because his customers were satisfied and the shy ones and the retiring ones and the irresolute ones left the premises safe in the knowledge that they would not be laughed at because of their choice of head-gear.

As time passed and it became clear that the union would not be blessed with children Polly Baun became known as the woman who hated Christmas. Nobody would ever say it to her face and certainly nobody would say it to her husband's face. It must be said on behalf of the community that none took real exception to her stance. They were well used to Christmas attitudes. There was a tradesman who resided in the suburbs and every year about a week before Christmas he would disappear into the countryside where he rented a small cabin until Christmas was over. He had nothing personal against Christmas and had said so publicly on numerous occasions. It was just that he couldn't stand the build-up to Christmas what with the decorations and the lighting and the cards and the shopping and the gluttony to mention but a few of his grievances.

There was another gentleman who locked his door on Christmas Eve and did not open it for a month. Some say he simply hibernated and when he reappeared on the street after the prescribed period he looked as if he had. He was unshaven and his hair was tousled and his face was gaunt as a corpse's and there were black circles under his eyes.

Then there were those who would go off the drink for Christmas just because everybody else was going on. And there were those who would not countenance seasonal fare such as turkeys or geese or plum pudding or spiced beef. One man said he would rather an egg and another insisted that those who consumed fowl would have tainted innards for the rest of their days.

There were, therefore, abundant precedents for attitudes like Polly Baun's. There were those who would excuse her on the grounds that maybe she had a good and secret reason to hate Christmas but mostly they would accept what Shaun said, that she simply discouraged it.

There had been occasions when small children would come to the door of the kitchen while their parents searched for suitable hats. The knowing ones would point to where the silhouette of the woman who hated Christmas was visible through the stained glass of the doorway which led from the shop to the kitchen. One might whisper to the others as he pointed inwards 'that's the woman who hates Christmas!' If Polly heard, she never reacted. Sometimes in the streets, during the days before Christmas, she would find herself the object of curious stares from shoppers who had just been informed of her pet aversion by friends or relations. If she noticed she gave no indication.

Shaun also felt the seasonal undercurrents when he visited his neighbourhood tavern during the Christmas festivities. He drank but little, a few glasses of stout with a friend but never whiskey. He had once been a prodigious whiskey drinker and then all of a sudden he gave up whiskey altogether and never indulged again. No one knew why, not even his closest friends. There was no explanation. One night he went home full of whiskey and the next night he drank none. There was the inevitable speculation but the truth would never be known and his friends, all too well aware of his fiery temper, did not pursue the matter. Neither did they raise the question of his wife's Christmas disposition except when his back was turned but like most of the community they did not consider it to be of any great significance. There was, of course, a reason for it. There had to be if one accepted the premise that there was a reason for everything.

On Christmas Eve there was much merriment and goodwill in the tavern. Another of Shaun Baun's cronies had given up whiskey on his doctor's instructions and presumed wrongly that this might well have been the reason why Shaun had forsaken the stuff. Courteously but firmly Shaun informed him that his giving up whiskey had nothing to do with doctors, that it was a purely personal decision. The night was spoiled for Shaun Baun. Rather than betray his true feelings on such an occasion he slipped away early and walked as far as the outermost suburbs of the town, then turned and made his way homewards at a brisk pace. Nobody could be blamed for thinking that here was a busy shopkeeper availing himself of the rarer airs of the night whereas the truth was that his mind was in turmoil, all brought on by the reference to whiskey in the public house. Nobody knew better than Shaun why he had given up whiskey unless it was his wife.

As he walked he clenched and unclenched his fists and cursed the day that he had ever tasted whiskey. He remembered striking her and he remembered why and as he did he stopped and threw his arms upwards into the night and sobbed as he always sobbed whenever he found himself unable to drive the dreadful memory away. He remembered how he had been drinking since the early afternoon on that fateful occasion. Every time he sold a hat he would dash across the roadway to the pub with the purchaser in tow. He reckoned afterwards that he had never consumed so much whiskey in so short a time. When he closed the shop he announced that he was going straight to the public house and this despite his wife's protestations. She begged him to eat something. She lovingly entreated him not to drink any more whiskey, to indulge in beer or stout and he agreed and kissed her and then hurried off to surfeit himself with more whiskey. He would later excuse himself on the grounds that he was young and impetuous but he would never be able to excuse the use of his fist in that awful moment which would haunt him for the rest of his life. An oncoming pedestrian moved swiftly on to the roadway at the sight of the gesticulating creature who seemed to rant and rave as he approached. Shaun Baun moved relentlessly onward, trying to dispel the memory of what had been the worst moment he had ever experienced but he still remembered as though it had happened only the day before.

He had left the pub with several companions and they had gone on to an after-hours establishment where they exceeded themselves. Shaun had come home at seven o'clock in the morning. He searched in vain for his key but it was nowhere to be found. He turned out his pockets but the exercise yielded nothing. Then he did what his likes had been doing since the first key had been mislaid. He knocked gently upon the front window with his knuckles and when this failed to elicit a response he located a coin and used it to beat a subdued tattoo on the fanlight and when this failed he pounded upon the door.

At length the door was opened to him and closed behind him by his dressing-gowned, bedroom-slippered wife. It took little by way of skill to evade his drunken embrace. She passed him easily in the shop and awaited him with folded arms in the kitchen.

A wiser woman would have ushered him upstairs, bedded him safely down and suspended any verbal onslaught until a more favourable time. She did not know so early in her married days that the most futile of all wifely exercises is arguing with a drunken husband.

She began by asking him if he saw the state of himself which was a pointless question to begin with. She asked him in short order if he knew the hour of the morning it was and was he aware of the fact that he was expected to accompany her to mass in a few short hours. He stood silently, hands and head hanging, unable to muster a reply. All he wished for was his bed; even the floor would have satisfied him but she had only begun. She outlined for him all the trouble he had caused her in their three years of marriage, his drinking habits, his bouts of sickness after the excesses of the pub, his intemperate language and, worst of all, the spectacle he made of himself in front of the neighbours. Nothing remarkable here, the gentle reader would be sure to say, familiar enough stuff and common to such occasions in the so-called civilised countries of the world but let me stress that it was not the quality of her broadsides but the quantity. She went on and on and on and it became clear that she should have vented her ire piecemeal over the three years rather than hoard it all for one sustained outburst.

Afterwards Shaun Baun would say that he did what he did to shut out the noise. If there had been lulls now and then he might have borne it all with more patience but she simply never let up. On the few occasions that he nodded off she shouted into the more convenient ear so that he would splutter into immediate if drunken wakefulness. Finally, the whole business became unbearable. Her voice had reached its highest pitch since the onslaught began and she even grew surprised at the frenzy of her own outpourings.

Could she but have taken a leaf out of the books of the countless wives in the neighbourhood who found themselves confronted with equally intemperate spouses she would have fared much better and there would be no need for recrimination on Christmas morning. Alas, this was not her way. She foolishly presumed that the swaying monstrosity before her was one of a kind and that a drastic dressing-down of truly lasting proportions was his only hope of salvation.

Whenever he tried to move out of earshot she seized him firmly by the shoulders and made him stand his ground.

Drunk and incapable as he was he managed to place the table between them. For awhile they played a game of cat and mouse but eventually he tired and she began a final session of ranting which had the effect of clouding his judgment such was its intensity. He did not realise that he had delivered the blow until she had fallen to the ground.

Afterwards he would argue with himself that he only meant to remove her from his path so that he could escape upstairs and find succour in the spare bedroom. She fell heavily, the blood streaming from a laceration on her cheekbone. When he attempted to help her he fell awkwardly across her and stunned himself when his forehead struck the floor. When he woke he saw that the morning's light was streaming in the window. The clock on the kitchen mantelpiece confirmed his worst fears. For the first time in his life he had missed mass. Then slowly the events of the night before began to take shape. He prayed in vain that he had experienced a nightmare, that his wife would appear any moment bouncing and cheerful from last mass. He struggled to his feet and entered his shop.

The last of the mass-goers had departed the street outside. Fearing the worst he climbed the stairs to the bedroom which they had so lovingly shared since they first married. She lay on the bed her head propped up by bloodstained pillows, a plaster covering the gash she had suffered, her face swollen beyond belief. Shaun fell on his knees at the side of the bed and sobbed his very heart out but the figure on the bed lay motionless, her unforgiving eyes fixed on the ceiling. There would be no Christmas dinner on that occasion. Contritely, all day and all night, he made sobbing visitations to the bedroom with cups of coffee and tea and other beverages but there was to be no relenting.

Three months would pass before she acknowledged his existence and three more would expire before words were exchanged. Two years in all would go unfleetingly by before it could be said that they had the semblance of a relationship. That had all been twenty-five years before and now as he walked homewards avoiding the main streets he longed to kneel before her and beg her forgiveness once more. Every so often during the course of every year in between he would ask her to forgive the unforgivable as he called it. He had never touched her in anger since that night or raised his voice or allowed his face to exhibit the semblance of a frown in her presence.

When he returned she was sitting silently by the fire. The goose, plucked and stuffed, sat on a large dish. It would be duly roasted on the morrow. As soon as he entered the kitchen he sat by her side and took her hand in his. As always, he declared his love for her and she responded, as always, by squeezing the hand which held hers. They would sit thus as they had sat since that unforgettable night so many years before. There would be no change in the pattern. They would happily recall the events of the day and they would decide upon which mass they would attend on the great holy day. She would accept the glass of sherry which he always poured for her. He would pour himself a bottle of stout and they would sip happily. They would enjoy another drink and another and then they would sit quietly for awhile. Then as always the sobbing would begin. It would come from deep within him. He would kneel in front of her with his head buried in her lap and every so often, between great heaving sobs, he would tell her how sorry he was. She would nod and smile and place her hands around his head and then he would raise the head and look into her eyes and ask her forgiveness as he had been doing for so many years.

'I forgive you dear,' she would reassure him and he would sob all the more. She would never hurt him. She could not find it in her heart to do that. He was a good man if a hotheaded one and he had made up for that moment of madness many times over. All through the night she would dutifully comfort him by accepting his every expression of atonement. She always thought of her father on such occasions. He had never raised his voice to her or to her mother. He had been drunk on many an occasion, notably weddings and christenings but all he ever did was to lift her mother or herself in his arms. She was glad that she was able to forgive her husband but there was forgiveness and forgiveness and hers was the kind that would never let her forget. Her husband would never know the difference. She would always be there when he needed her, especially at Christmas.

9
PROTOCOL

I could tell from the expression on Timmy Binn's face that he had come down from the hilltop on a special mission. Most times he called merely to pass away the winter nights. He would sit by the hearth with my uncle and his wife and maybe her father if the old man felt up to it. There they would exchange news and views until midnight when the party broke up after a cup or two of tea.

Mȳ uncle's house sat snugly in the lee of a small Sitka spruce plantation at the bottom of the hill whereas the Binn abode was almost at the top about a mile distant. At the time Timmy Binn was approaching his seventieth year which made him the youngest of three bachelor brothers and three spinster sisters who lived together in their ancient farmhouse which looked down on every other in the parish.

The isolation suited the Binns. They were seen in public by early morning mass-goers only. These, for the most part, would be old and retiring like themselves, venturing forth weekly to the village church in order to observe the Sabbath.

Timmy it was who did all the shopping. Every morning, Sunday included, he tackled the old black mare to the milk cart and guided her to the creamery with the tanks containing the daily yield from the twelve milch cows. When the milk was delivered he would purchase the necessary provisions and return home without further delay.

On Fridays he collected the several old age pensions due to his brothers and sisters at the village post office. Half of the money was spent on luxuries like coil tobacco, snuff and mixed fruit jam. The other half was credited to a joint account in a well worn post office book. This was left untouched over the years so that it might meet wake and funeral expenses when, one by one, the Binns would be faced with the ultimate contingency.

'Come up to the fire,' my uncle called as soon as the door was closed.

Timmy's mouth opened to say something but he thought better of it and sat by the fire as instructed.

'You'll take a bottle of porter,' the uncle said. 'In fact,' said he before Timmy could answer, 'we'll all take a bottle of porter.'

Normally Timmy Binn would have been offered tea but Christmas was not long past and there still remained some bottled porter after the festivities. The uncle uncorked three bottles. He handed one to Timmy and another to his father-in-law. The third he kept for himself. No glasses were used.

'Sláinte,' said the uncle as he lifted the bottle to his mouth.

'Sláinte,' the others answered and they did likewise.

Each went halfway down and as soon as Timmy Binn had placed his on the floor at the side of his chair he readied himself to make an announcement. None came however. From where I sat reading at the kitchen table I could see that he was under great strain. He wanted to come out with something but couldn't. I was about to intervene and say 'Let Timmy talk', but I remembered that it was the custom to exhaust every other topic before asking for the reason behind any visit. I remembered that Timmy had arrived only a few weeks before on an errand for his sisters. He had spent nearly two hours talking in front of the hearth with my uncle and the old man. Finally when he was handed a cup of tea by the woman of the house he announced that he would not have time to drink it. He explained that he had been sitting in his own kitchen while his sisters were preparing supper when they suddenly discovered that there wasn't a grain of sugar in the house. Timmy had been dispatched straightaway for the loan of a cupful till morning. He nevertheless allowed himself to be coerced into drinking the tea on the grounds that his sisters would have gone ahead with the supper anyway in view of his long absence.

This time, however, an uncharacteristic agitation showed. He fussed and fidgeted but restrained himself, remembering that there was a ritual to be observed. Neither my uncle nor the old man commented on his restlessness. They presumed that he would withhold the reason for his visit as a matter of course until such time as he was asked. They knew quite well that he had come for a purpose other than sitting and talking but part of the proceedings consisted of endeavouring to deduce in their own minds precisely what that purpose was. The whole undertaking would be spoiled if he came out with his business straight-off. It mattered not how pressing that business might be nor did it count that he might be in a hurry back home. Tradition obliged him to sit it out until the proper time.

'There are poor people sheltering this night without a fire.'

The old man of the house swallowed the remainder of his stout after he had spoken. He handed the empty bottle to my uncle in such a manner as to suggest that the opening of three more bottles might not be inappropriate.

'A good blaze is everything,' his daughter said, lovingly laying three large black sods on the perimeter of the fire, 'and I'll tell you what is more,' she went on, 'a good fire will draw pain out of a body.'

'Tuck, tuck,' her father said in agreement.

The uncapped bottles were handed out again and the menfolk quaffed. A lengthy silence followed during which Timmy Binn stirred uneasily in his chair. My uncle and the old man exchanged knowing glances.

'We're on a big one this time,' the old man's expression spoke for him.

'No doubt about that,' Timmy's said.

The silence continued. They were searching for clues, putting together bits and pieces of information from the happenings of the previous weeks. Something out of the ordinary had happened at Binn's, something not quite calamitous but yet important enough to make an easy-going hillman like Timmy Binn uneasy and fidgety.

'I mind worse winters nor this,' the old man spoke to relieve the tension.

'Tell us about the time of the big snow,' his daughter urged.

'I was only a boy then,' the old man began.

We had heard the story twenty times but it was well suited to a winter's night and it always improved in the retelling. Even Timmy Binn seemed to forget his assignment as the tale unfolded. All the while the wind howled in the chimney and now and then a shower of passing hailstones beat furiously on the windows. The narrative ended after a half hour with the old man declaring that he needed a drop of something stronger than common porter to restore his flagging energy.

'Storytelling is dry work.' This was a favourite saying of his. Without a word his daughter removed herself and returned a moment later with a bottle of whiskey.

'I was keeping it for an occasion,' she explained, 'but I suppose this is as good an occasion as any.'

She too sensed that Timmy was the bearer of exceptional tidings. The whiskey was her contribution to the prolongment. A woman less sensitive to the lifestyle of the countryside might have terminated the programme there and then by simply doing nothing.

'Any sign of snow up your way, Timmy?' The uncle tendered the spirits and the question at the same time.

'The odd flake is all I've seen so far,' Timmy answered.

'The odd flake eh?' The old man pondered the response as he searched for further questions in his whiskey glass. Failing to find any he lifted it to his lips and skilfully tossed a dollop into his mouth where he allowed it to remain for a while before swallowing it with great relish. It provided him with the inspiration he needed. He was activated by an almost imperceptible spasm as the whiskey reached its destination. He nodded appreciatively.

'Right on target,' he said to nobody in particular. 'If the first shot hits the bullseye,' he declared, 'then all the other shots will do the same. It is vital, therefore, to hold the whiskey under your tongue until the stomach is ready to receive it. People don't know how to drink whiskey anymore. Nowadays they swallow it back like it was water and they're paralysed drunk before they know it.'

For a quarter hour he held forth on the subject of whiskey drinking. Whether it was the porter or the whiskey or both, Timmy Binn had more or less resigned himself to the situation. He looked blankly into the fire as the old man roamed aimlessly over a wide field of topics. The uncle took over just as it seemed his father-in-law must topple into sleep from sheer verbal exhaustion. The uncle lacked the narrative skills of the old man but he, nevertheless, managed to contain the visitor with the sheer forcefulness of his dialogue. All the while the old man nodded drowsily but yet managed to stay awake. His daughter sat nearer to him so as to act as a prop whenever he leaned sideways. The uncle supported him on the other side.

Silently I went out of doors. The hail had stopped. The roadway had a bleached look. On the hilltop the Binn farmhouse was ablaze with light. I half expected to see one of the brothers descending the narrow roadway in search of Timmy but the hill road was empty. Undoubtedly there was something amiss at the top of the hill. Up until this time there had been but a single faint light to indicate the whereabouts of the Binn habitation. Now there was this unprecedented radiance shimmering outrageously in the lofty distance like a newly transfixed star of great magnitude. It outshone every other light in the countryside. Then a fleeting cloud obscured the moon and total darkness fell on the roadway. I hurried back to the house. Before going in I looked through the window into the kitchen. The old man's head dropped as he sat squeezed upright by his daughter and the uncle. She occupied herself with the darning of a sock nodding in assent at the observations being made by her husband. For his part he sat with flushed face and held forth for all he was worth using his long arms to stress the elements of his narrative that needed stressing. His mouth opened and closed with great rapidity. It seemed a grim tale indeed but it had little effect on the visitor.

Timmy Binn sat with his legs outstretched, his head forward on his chest as though he had been hypnotised, his empty glass cupped loosely in his grimy hand looking as if it must fall to the floor at any moment. Then the uncle suddenly finished his talk and twiddled his thumbs.

'What's the night like outside?' He asked the question as soon as I had reoccupied my chair.

'Black as pitch,' I answered.

'You won't get blacker than that.' This affirmation was addressed to Timmy Binn who emerged slowly out of his trance.

'What was that?' he asked apologetically.

'It don't matter,' the uncle reassured him.

'Anyone on the road?' the woman of the house asked.

'Not a living Christian,' I answered, 'except that there is a fierce light on the hilltop.'

The lethargy which held sway for so long suddenly disappeared. Everybody was attentive.

'What part of the hill?' the uncle asked.

'Where Binn's is,' I answered, as casually as I could.

'Where Binn's is?' It was the old man coming into his own once more. This was the moment for which Timmy Binn had waited all night. Every eye was now turned upon him. His time had come at long last. A total of two and a half hours had passed since he first set foot in the kitchen. He placed his glass on the floor between his legs and folded his hands over his stomach waiting for the question that was to be his cue. It was posed by the old man.

'And pray Timmy,' he said innocently, 'what business brought you down from the hill this night?'

'I would be wanting the loan of six or eight chairs,' said Timmy Binn.

'Why would you be wanting six or eight chairs?' It was the uncle's turn now.

'Because,' said Timmy Binn, 'one of us is dead and we're short of chairs for the wake.'

A brief silence ensued during which the uncle and the old man exchanged I-told-you-so glances. They had guessed right. They had been on a big one. The wait had been worthwhile and despite the importance of the mission due protocol had been observed. That was what really mattered.

10
'YOU'RE ON NEXT SUNDAY'

You'll find more than a few to tell you that there isn't a word
of truth in the following story and the nearer you come to the
place where it happened you'll find a lot more. When I taxed
the man who told me the story with these facts he took his pipe
from his mouth, spat into the fire and looked me between the
eyes for an embarrassingly long spell. He did not speak but
when he returned the pipe to his mouth I knew that the tale
was true and that those who belied it were either knaves or
fools.

It happened on the fifteenth day of August in the year of
our Lord, as they say in these parts, 1934. It was a fair year for
primroses, a better one for hay and a woeful year for funerals.

'The Fifteenth' as it is still called locally is the annual
Pattern Day in the lovely seaside resort of Ballybunion. From
all quarters of Kerry, Cork and Limerick would come thousands of country people in every mode of conveyance from bike
to omnibus to shanks' mare and pony cart. They still come but
in nothing like the vast numbers of yore.

That particular Fifteenth, as I recall, broke fair and clear.
Skies were blue. The air was fresh and wholesome and there
was a hearty trace of fine breeze from the west. At the cream-
eries and dispensaries that morning man, woman and child
wore happy faces.

''Tis a great day for the Fifteenth,' they would say to each other and back would come the reply, 'ah sure 'tis a great day entirely.' At quarter to eleven in the noon of the day my grand-uncle Morrisheen Digley went forth to the haggard to catch the pony and at the turn of the noon he set forth for Ballybunion in his newly varnished trap. It would do your heart good to see the dancing legs of the pony and the squinting sparks on the flinty road when his iron-shod hooves made light of the long haul. I did not go on the occasion. He said I was too young. Instead he called for his old crony Thady Dowd of Lacca. Neither of the two was under seventy but none gamer set out that day for Ballybunion.

They untackled the pony in the back yard of Mikey Joe's Irish-American Bar and celebrated their arrival at the Pattern with two glasses of potstill whiskey. This was followed by a brace of pints, pints of creamy black porter. These were con-sumed so that the remains of the whiskey might be entirely scoured from the gullet, a most advisable practice this if one is to believe those who are fond of indulging in such procedural drinking.

Towards evening they walked as far as the beach to savour the salt sea air and to partake of a paddle near the shore. According to the old people there was nothing the equal of a paddle in the salt water to cure what might be wrong with you. It was pleasant on the shore. The fresh Atlantic breeze was sharp and bracing but as yet without its late autumnal sting. There were hundreds like themselves pacing up and down, ankle deep in the water, content to dawdle aimlessly until the anxiety for drink returned.

In the village they met neighbours from the townland of Lacca and between them they started a singsong in one of the public houses. When darkness fell a great hunger for meat seized them. They repaired to a café where they were served with succulent steaks and roast potatoes. This was followed by two dishes of rich trifle and the lot was washed down by several cups of strong, well-sugared tea.

'This will make a handy base for more drink,' my granduncle announced to Thady Dowd. Dowd nodded agreement happily. So far the pair had enjoyed themselves thoroughly and the night was still but a starry-eyed child in swaddling clothes. The best was to come. After the meal they embarked on a grand tour of the village pubs and had a drink in every one.

At this stage the reader will begin to raise an eyebrow or two and wonder what is the purpose in the retelling of such a commonplace narrative. Was not their visit to the Pattern but a replica of other years, a common jaunt indulged in by thousands of others and all following the same predictable course?

Patience dear reader and bear with me. As soon as the time came to close the pubs three pairs of well-made civic guards appeared on the street and by their presence ensured that every tavern was cleared. The publicans were grateful enough for theirs had been a long and arduous day. By this stage Thady Dowd and my granduncle had more than their share of strong drink but for the purpose of shortening the road home they invested in a half pint of whiskey apiece at Mikey Joe's American Bar.

Earlier they had plied the pony with a sufficiency of oats and when they came to tackle him they found him in excellent fettle. Like all animals who have spent a long day away from the green pastures of home he was full of taspy for the task before him. As soon as he found the open road free from obstacles he started to trot in real earnest. Overhead a full moon lit up the countryside and the sky, its full complement of stars visible in all its quarters, shone like a treasure-house. In the body of the trap the semi-drunken companions sang at the top of their voices to the steady accompaniment of the pony's clopping hooves.

They sang song after song and from time to time they would uncork their whiskey bottles and partake of wholesome slugs. This made them sing all the louder and soon every dog in the countryside was responding. There was an unholy cacophony as the miles fell behind them.

Then, suddenly, for no reason whatsoever the pony stopped in his tracks and despite their most earnest entreaties would not be coaxed into moving a single, solitary inch.

'What's the matter with the creature anyway?' Thady Dowd asked indignantly.

'Beats me,' said my granduncle.

All around there was an unearthly silence save for the chuckling of the Gale River which lay just ahead of them spanned by a narrow bridge. It was the same Gale that poor Spenser the poet did not forget when he wrote about Irish rivers. On the left the crosses and tombstones of Gale church-yard stood pale and grey in the drenching moonlight. The pony stood rooted to the roadway, head bent, his whole frame taut and tense. There was white foam at the corners of his mouth and a look of abject terror, terrible to behold, in his bloodshot eyes.

'I don't like the look of things,' my granduncle whispered.

'A rattling damn I don't give,' Dowd shouted, 'I'm getting out of here to see what the matter is.'

'Stay as you are,' my granduncle counselled but there was no stopping the headstrong Dowd. He jumped on to the roadway and walked round trap and pony several times.

'There's nothing here,' he called out. He then proceeded towards the river thinking that some calamity might have overtaken the bridge and that the pony, with its animal instinct, might have sensed this. The bridge was in perfect order. Dowd looked over its twin parapets into the shallow, warbling water. He could see nothing unusual.

He retraced his steps and with a scornful toss of his grey head went towards the graveyard of Gale. As soon as he entered the little byroad which led to the gateway the pony lifted its head and followed slowly. It is well to remember that at no time did my granduncle leave the trap. He sat stiffly, holding the reins, carefully following his friend's every move.

When Dowd leaned across the gate of the graveyard he emitted a loud yell of genuine surprise. There before him were two hurling teams dressed in togs, jerseys and slippers. Every hurler had a hurley in his hand and at one side sitting on a low tombstone sat a small inoffensive-looking, bald-headed man. He wore a white jersey as distinct from the two teams who wore red and green respectively. He had a sliotar or hurley ball in one hand and in the other he held an ancient, burnished, copper hunting horn.

The pony had stopped dead a second time opposite the gateway over which Dowd was leaning.

'Come away out of that,' my granduncle called out, 'and leave the dead to themselves.'

'What's the use?' Dowd called back, 'the pony won't budge till it suits these people.'

'What's the matter,'he called out to the hurlers who stood about as if they were waiting for something special to happen. At first no one heeded him but when he called out belligerently a second time a tall player with a face the colour of lime-stone approached the gate. He explained to Dowd that he was the captain of the red-jerseyed hurlers but that the game could not start because his team was short a man.

'Who are these teams anyway?' Dowd asked cheekily.

The captain explained that his team was Ballyduff and the other team Ballybawn.

'Ho-ho,' cried Dowd exultantly. 'I'm your man. My mother, God be good to her, was a Ballyduff woman. If you have no objection I will play with your team.'

The captain nodded silently and when my granduncle called to Dowd to abandon his arrant foolishness the captain turned and addressed him where he sat in the trap.

'Not an inch will you or your pony move,' said he in a hollow, haunted voice, 'until the final horn is sounded in this game of hurling.'

My granduncle said no more. The pony stood now like a statue and the sounds of the river were no longer to be heard. Overhead the moon shone brightly and the pitch which was the length and breadth of the graveyard, was illuminated as though it were floodlit. Forms appeared from the ground and sat themselves on the graveyard wall. The referee looked up-wards at the moon and after a few moments wait blew upon the hunting horn. Then he threw in the ball.

The exchanges started slowly enough with Dowd's team, Ballyduff, getting the worst of it from a faster Ballybawn side. The first score came when the referee awarded a free puck to Ballybawn. He also cautioned a number of the Ballyduff play-ers, notably Dowd and the captain, for abusive language to-wards himself and for dirty play in general.

The Ballybawn skipper drove the ball straight between the

uprights. On the graveyard walls the partisans went wild and a fist fight broke out near the gate. Somebody flung an empty cocoa canister at the referee and he threatened to call off the game if the crowd did not behave themselves. There were a number of fistic exchanges on the field of play but by and large the standard of hurling was as good as my granduncle had seen for many a day. There were many fluent movements and excellent long-range scores. The wrist work and pulling left little to be desired. Half time came and went and now the two teams were playing for all they were worth. Time was slipping away and with five minutes to go the sides were level.

Neither would yield an inch. Every player strove manfully to register the single score that would put his own team ahead of the other. The ghostly forms jumped up and down on the walls egging the players on to greater deeds.

It seemed as if the game must end in a draw and the granduncle noted that from time to time the referee looked nervously at the full moon and feverishly fingered his hunting horn, anxious for full time to roll round so that he might wash his hands of the whole affair. There is nothing a referee loves so dearly as a drawn game. The hopes of both sides are kept alive and it is unlikely that he will be assaulted as he leaves the pitch. With less than a minute remaining there was a mêlée at midfield in which Dowd was involved. Fists flew and hurleys were raised. More than once could be heard the clash of ash against dougthy skulls.

The referee intervened and taking a scroll from his togs' pocket he commenced the business of taking names. It was during this lull that Dowd sat on a convenient tombstone to savour a richly-merited breather. He withdrew the half pint bottle from his trousers pocket and dolefully surveyed the remnants of his whiskey. The bottle was still quarter full. He raised it to his lips and without once taking it from his head swallowed the contents. Almost immediately he heaved a great sigh which could be heard all over the graveyard. Then he tightened his trousers' belt and waited for play to resume.

With seconds remaining the hunting horn was sounded yet again and the ball was thrown in. Dowd it was who won possession. With a fierce and drunken yell he cut through his opponents like a scythe through switch-grass with the ball poised on the base of his hurley. There were times when he darted like a trout and times when he bounded like a stag. He leaped over grave mounds and skirted crosses and tombstones at breakneck speed. All the time he edged his way nearer the opposing goal line.

Seeing an opening on the left wing he seized his chance and headed straight for the goal with the entire Ballybawn team on his heels like a pack of hungry hounds. Thirty yards out he stopped dead and took a shot. The ball went away to the right but if it did it passed through the eye of a Celtic cross and rebounded off the head of a plaster angel. The rebound was deflected towards the goal by the extended hand of the figure of Michael the Archangel. It skeeved the left upright and found its way to the back of the net.

Need I mention that while the ball was travelling so was the empty whiskey bottle which Dowd, with sound foresight, had flung at the Ballybawn goalkeeper as soon as the referee's back was turned. The crowd went wild. The Ballyduff team and supporters milled around Dowd and embraced him. Then they lifted him aloft and trotted round the graveyard on a lap of victory. Finishing the lap the Ballyduff captain called for three cheers for their visitor. Three eerie ullagones went heavenwards and died slowly till the muted river sounds took over once more. The teams had suddenly vanished save for the tall, ghostly presence of the Ballyduff captain. For the first time in over an hour the pony stirred. He pawed the dirt boreen, anxious for the high road.

'Come on at once,' my granduncle called. Dowd, escorted by the captain, made his way towards the gate where the pony was now prancing and difficult to restrain. Dowd shook hands with the captain and was about to depart when a ghostly hand was laid firmly on his right shoulder. The captain leaned forward and whispered into Dowd's ear. Whatever it was he said Dowd's face underwent a terrible change. The glowing red nose was now puce-coloured and the rosy, whiskey-tinted cheeks were ashen grey. Slowly, almost painfully, he climbed across the gate while the captain faded like a breeze-driven mist behind him.

In the trap Dowd was silent and thoughtful. On his face was a woebegone look that struck a chill in my granduncle's heart. The pony highstepped his way homewards, his dark mane flowing loosely behind him, his firm rump bobbing up and down as the miles passed by.

Finally my granduncle popped the question.

'What in heaven's name did he say to you?' he asked.

Dowd shook his head sadly before he replied. The he spoke slowly and deliberately with a crack in his voice.

'He informed me,' Dowd announced, 'that because of the way I played tonight I would be on for good next Sunday.'

11
THE FORT FIELD

'Grass for ten cows and water for a million!' The old man laughed when he said it.

It was a long time ago. We were driving the cows down the bohareen for the evening milking. We were in a hurry. There was to be a football game that evening in Castleisland. A Tralee team was coming and there was talk of a needle. Through the yellow whins that stood out against the green hedges I could see his small fields, some still glinting sogginess in the height of summer.

'There's a play here,' I told myself. The old man is the hero and his wife is the heroine. The ten cows and the other live-stock are the characters all but one. I am the chorus. You notice I leave the villain till last. Yet he was there from the very beginning. He is the water, the ever-present, the everlasting, the accursed water.

The old man used to boast good-humouredly in public houses that a man on horseback could not ride round the whole of his farm in a day. Strangers would shake their heads in incredulity but those who knew his terrain would wait patiently for the explanatory foot note.

''Tis true for me,' the old man would say. 'Horse and rider would be drowned after the Fort Field.'

As we neared the white-washed cow-stall, next to the dwelling-house at the little road's end, we leaned over the five-bar gate to look into this field. It was a special place with a character of its own, snug as a carpeted parlour with a green more vivid than any of its neighbours. It was covered with good quality clover and natural vetches, the kind of field the man above makes especially to compensate for all the other squelchy, boggy acres. In spite of the fact that it was surrounded by inferior pastures it yet managed to remain aloof. It was similar in appearance to the excellent land one sees through a train window as one nears Dublin and I often asked myself what it was doing in the middle of total strangers.

It was so-called because of an ancient redan which occupied its furthest corner with its apex facing towards the gate. There were many such archaic redoubts in the district, but none had the purpose or individuality of this particular one.

The field comprised one acre, one rood and thirty-two perches. Needless to mention, it was pampered. It was conceded more cartloads of dung than any of the others and it was well-supported with annual investments of lime. Nothing was too good for it. It was the best-drained on the whole farm and I suspect it was a showpiece.

In spite of our hurry we lingered at the gate. I knew he would make no move until I spoke. I knew what was expected of me. I climbed onto one of the concrete piers and donned my admiration look.

'That's a powerful parcel of land,' I said after a little while.

To this he made no reply, but from his even breathing I knew I had registered.

''Tis as fine a bit of land,' I went on, 'as you'd find if you footed it from Portmagee to Tarbert Island.'

He patted a passing cow on the rump but said nothing. This was to show how modest he was. He always pretended he didn't care.

'It's a field,' I said, 'fit for a racehorse.'

He spoke then, for the first time.

"Tisn't bad,' he admitted. "Tisn't the worst anyhow.'

For a man who was supposed to be in a hurry he showed little inclination towards getting a move on. I knew I had better bring things to a close; otherwise we might miss the football game. I had to end on the highest possible note and so I racked my brain for a conclusive compliment. He was expecting it. He tapped one foot impatiently.

"Tis a land worth fighting for,' I said suddenly, remembering the phrase from a school book.

'That's good,' he said, repeating the words after me.

'A land worth fighting for. That's very good indeed.' As we walked down the road he took a shilling from his pocket and handed it to me. The shilling was owing to me in the first place but I didn't think it would come so soon. After the cows were milked there was another surprise. This time it was for the cows. Instead of turning them into the inches by the small river I was instructed to allow them into the Fort Field. They truly appreciated the gesture for when I opened the gate they thundered past me, bellowing delightedly with their tails cocked high.

In Castleisland when the football game was over we repaired to a public house. Country folk, in those days, would leave their custom with traders who hailed originally from their own part of the world, so that when a farmer's son set up a business in a nearby town he could be sure of the support of the folk who came from his own townland and thereabouts.

Men who stand behind the bars of public houses have to be diplomatic or go broke. The publican we visited was no exception. At one time he had been a neighbour of the old man's. His greeting was warm and tactful and when he had dried his hands with a cloth he extended one to each of us in turn.

'How're the men?' was the first thing he said. This was clever because not only did it embrace us both but it gave me a dimension for which all boys long. I liked him immediately but when he winked at me and pulled upon his waxed moustache my heart went out to him altogether.

Our drinks were ordered, delivered almost at once, and paid for.

'Did you start cutting yet?' the publican asked.

'Indeed I did not,' the old man replied, 'but if this fine spell continues it could well be that I might be tempted.'

'There's a lot of hay down,' a listener put in.

'Meadows are light,' the old man countered. 'It's nothing but vanity.'

Talk ebbed and flowed. The bar began to fill and as time went by the speeches grew longer and a little louder. Men who were silent earlier could not be deterred from commenting on any and all subjects that came up for discussion.

All round us post-mortems on the game were in full swing.

'You'll never beat a Tralee team while the ball is dry,' a man with a pipe in his hand pointed out.

'That may be,' said another, 'but I tell you that Castleisland should have made more use of the wings. When you play the wings you draw the backs and when you draw the backs you get the openings.'

When there was a lull in trade the publican returned to us. He leaned out over the high counter.

'How many cows are you milking presently?' he asked.

'Ten,' the old man answered.

'Any heifers?'

'Two.'

'Calves?'

'Four.'

It was plain to see that he had little relish for this sort of conversation. It was altogether too banal and unlikely to strike an interesting note.

'That's a nice field,' the publican tried a new tack, 'the one with the five-bar gate and the old fort in it.'

Immediately the old man sat bolt upright. The conversation had taken a turn to his liking. The publican, realising he had scored, pressed home his advantage.

'You could sleep on it,' he said, 'and you wouldn't know the difference from a mattress.'

We were quite taken by this. The old man called for another drink. He included two countrymen who sat on stools beside us.

When farmers meet over a drink it is not to discuss art or politics and when they argue it is never about religion unless a parish priest is building a new church and is expecting a fixed amount per head of cattle. Farmers talk about the slips and stores and well-bred boars and when they elaborate, which is rarely, they mostly unfold on the theme of drainage grants or certified seed potatoes. Overall the talk would be of wet land and dry and when the Fort Field was thrust into the conversation it was inevitable that it would hold the limelight for a goodly spell.

'There is no field like it in this neck of the woods,' the old man announced.

The others nodded sagely and sipped their mediums of porter.

'And I don't mind tellin' you,' he went on, 'that a lot of folk I could mention has their eye on it.'

He submitted the latter part in undertone so that I wouldn't hear for I knew well that there was nobody interested in it but himself.

'I'm told,' said the publican, who had returned to us again, 'that if you searched it high and low in wintertime you would not find an eggcup of water in it.'

'Nor as much as would fill a thimble,' the old man supported.

This was followed by a long silence since nobody present could think of anything better to say and so pleasant was the atmosphere and so nicely turned the claims put forward that contradiction would have been sacrilegious. The talk flowed on like a soft stream and subjects from the warble fly to artificial manure were touched upon.

Then, out of the blue, the old man said to nobody in particular "Tis a land worth fighting for.'

All within earshot cocked their ears at the profundity of this and the two men who had joined us repeated the phrase lovingly lest it be damaged in transit from one mouth to another. Others, out of earshot originally, fastened on it secondhand and uttered it over and over to themselves and to others. The statement puzzled some and a few, not in the know, dismissed it altogether because they could not appreciate the significance of it. By and large it was well received and the majority, although they might never admit it, stored it away for use at some appropriate time in the future.

Before we realised it the time for closing had come. The publican struck the tall counter three times with a wooden mallet.

'Time for the road boys,' he said.

Without a word every man downed his drink and quietly we trooped out into the moonlight.

Later on, in bed, the sleep came quickly. It was good to stretch tired limbs on a soft feather tick. I have forgotten what time it was the old woman came into my room. All I recall is waking up to find her hand shaking my shoulder.

'What's up?' I asked drowsily.

'It's that cracked man of mine,' she complained. 'He can't sleep and wants you out a minute.'

I rose and went into the next room. He sat propped by pillows on the bed. His pipe was in his mouth and billows of smoke issued from between his clenched teeth.

'It's gone from me,' he said.

'What's gone from you?' I asked.

'What you said this evening about the Fort Field.'

'Oh that,' I laughed.

'It's no laughing matter,' he said crossly. 'I'm awake half the bloody night over it.'

"'Tis a land worth fighting for,' I reminded him.

He smiled at once and grasped the words as if they were his long lost brothers.

'Ah yes,' he said serenely and he placed his pipe on the bedside table. He flattened the pillows, lay back on the bed and drew the quilt under his chin. A smile of supreme content-ment transformed his face.

'A land worth fighting for,' he whispered half to himself. Then the snores came and he was deep in sleep.

12
THE CHANGE

The village slept. It was always half asleep. Now, because there was a flaming sun in the June sky, it was really asleep. It consisted of one long street with forty to fifty houses on either side. There were shops, far too many of them, and there were three decaying public houses the doors of which were closed as if they were ashamed to admit people. No, that isn't quite true. The truth is that passing strangers upset the tenor of normal life. The locals only drank at night, always sparingly, and were therefore reluctant to accept habits that conflicted with their own.

In the centre of the roadway a mangy Alsatian bitch sunned herself inconsiderately and that was all the life there was. The day was Friday. I remember it well because my uncle with whom I was staying had cycled to the pier earlier that morning for two fresh mackerel. Mackerel always taste better when they are cooked fresh.

Anyhow, the bitch lay stretched in the sun. From where I sat inside the window of my uncle's kitchen I could see the street from one end to the other. At nights when he didn't go to the pub that's what we would do; sit and watch the neighbours from the window. It was his place to comment and I would listen, dodging away to my room sometimes to write down something of exceptional merit. He was a great commentator but I never complimented him. He might stop if I did. It was hard, at times, to keep back the laughter although on rare occasions I was unable to smother it sufficiently and he would look at me suspiciously.

Behind me I could hear him in the kitchen. He made more noise than was strictly necessary.

'What way do you want it,' he called, 'boiled or fried?'

'Fried. Naturally.'

At the far end of the village a smart green sports car came into view. Its occupants were a boy and a girl. One minute the car was at the end of the street and the next it was braking furiously to avoid collision with the Alsatian bitch.

'What's happening out there?' But he didn't wait for my reply.

He was standing beside me with the frying pan in his hand. The car had stopped and the driver climbed out to remove the obstacle.

'Come on. Come on. Get up out a that, you lazy hound.'

Slowly the bitch turned over on her side and scratched the ranges of twin tits which covered her belly. She rose painfully and without looking at the driver slunk to the pavement where she immediately lay down again.

By this time a number of people stood in the door-ways of their houses. The squeal of brakes had penetrated the entire village and they had come to investigate. I followed my uncle to the doorway where we both stood silently watching the girl. She had eased herself from her seat and was now standing with hands on hips. She was tall and blonde. The tight-fitting red dress she wore clung to her body the way a label sticks to a bottle.

'Very nice. Very nice, indeed,' my uncle said.

'I think,' the girl told the driver, 'I'll take off this dress. I feel clammy.'

'Suit yourself,' he replied. With that he returned to his seat and lit a cigarette. The red dress was buttoned right down the front.

'What's the name of this place?' she asked as she ripped the topmost button. From the way she said it we knew that she couldn't care less.

'Don't know,' the driver said. Then, as an after-thought, 'don't care.'

She shrugged her slender shoulders and set to work on the other buttons, oblivious to the wide eyes and partly open mouths of the villagers. A door banged a few houses away but it was the only protest. When she reached the bottom buttons she was forced to stoop but she didn't grunt the way the village women did. Another shrug and the dress flowed from her to the ground.

Underneath she wore chequered shorts and a red bra, no more. The driver didn't even look when she asked him to hand her the sweater which was underneath her seat. Fumbling, his hand located the garment and he tossed it to her. He did make a comment however.

'Godsake hurry up,' he said with some irritation.

'Did you ever see such a heartless ruffian?' My uncle folded his arms and there was a dark look on his face. The girl stood for a moment or two shaking dust or motes or some such things from the sweater. Her whole body rippled at every movement. She started to pull the sweater over her head and then an astonishing thing happened. Nobody was prepared for it and this is probably why no one ever spoke about it afterwards. Everybody thought about it afterwards. I'm pretty certain of that.

Quite accidentally, I'm sure of that too, while she was adjusting her neck and shoulders so that she could the better accommodate the sweater, one of her breasts popped out into the sunlight. There were gasps. More doors banged.

A woman's voice called, 'Hussy. Hussy.'

Obviously she didn't hear. It was a deliciously pink living thing, dun-nippled and vital.

'Do 'em good,' my uncle whispered. 'Give 'em something to think about.'

The sweater in place, the girl adjusted her close-cropped hair. It didn't need adjusting but girls always seem to adjust their hair when it least needs it.

She picked up the dress and with her fingers felt the bonnet of the car. It must have been hot because she took the fingers away quickly and covered the bonnet with the dress. She then sat on the bonnet and from nowhere produced a tube of lipstick. All the while the driver sat looking straight in front of him. He threw the cigarette away before it had burned to the halfway stage. Now he sat with folded arms and hooded eyes that saw nothing.

The girl, her lips glistening, neatly folded the dress, went round to the boot of the car, flicked a button and tucked in the dress. Closing the boot she looked up and down the street. Her eyes scanned the few remaining faces with interest. If she noticed any reaction she did not show it in the least. For an instant her eyes met those of my uncle. He winked almost imperceptibly but she must have noticed it because she permitted herself the faintest glimmer of a smile as she entered the car. She punched the driver playfully and to give him his due he caught her round the shoulders and planted a swift kiss on the side of her face. Gears growled throatily and the car leaped forward into sudden life. In an instant it was gone and I was old enough to know that it had gone forever.

Later when we had eaten our mackerel we went to drive in the cows for the evening milking. This was the part of the day I liked best. The morning and afternoon hours dragged slowly and lamely but as soon as the evening milking was done there was the prospect of some excitement. We could cycle down to the pier and watch the lobster boats arriving home or we could go to the pub and listen.

On that particular evening we decided on the pub. Earlier while we were eating he had said that things would never be the same again. 'At least,' he confided, 'not for a hell of a long time anyway.' I had pressed him for an explanation.

'Look,' he said, 'I don't know exactly how to put it but that girl we saw changed things.'

'In what way?' I asked.

'Oh, damn,' he said, not unkindly, 'you have me addled. How do I know in what way? Is this the thanks I get for cooking your mackerel?'

'Aren't you afraid I'll grow up in ignorance?' He was fond of saying this when I failed to show interest in things he considered to be important. But he didn't rise to it. Instead he said: 'Wait and see. Wait and see, that's all.'

We went to the pub earlier than usual. He shaved before we left the house which was unusual for him. Most men in the village shaved only on Saturday nights or on the eve of holy days.

The pub was cool. There was a long wooden seat just inside the door. We sat and he called for a pint of stout and a bottle of lemonade. There were two other customers. One was a farmer's boy I knew by sight and the other was the young assistant teacher in the local boys' school.

'There was a lot of hay knocked today,' the publican said

when he had served the drinks and collected his money.

'There was indeed,' my uncle answered piously, 'and if this weather holds there will be a lot more knocked tomorrow.'

I gathered from this that he was at the top of his form. He was saying nothing out of the way. Nobody could possibly benefit from his words. He would go on all night like this relishing the utterly meaningless conversation.

The young teacher who was not a native of the place finished his drink and called for another. There was an unmistakable belligerence about him.

'A chip-carrier,' the uncle whispered, 'if ever I saw one.'

'What about the strip-tease act today?' the teacher ventured. When no one answered him he went to the window and looked out.

'Nothing ever happens here,' he pouted.

'True for you,' said the uncle.

He joined the teacher at the window. The three of us looked out into the street.

'Deserted,' the teacher said.

'Terrible,' from the uncle.

A couple came sauntering up the street.

'Here's up Flatface,' the teacher complained. Flatface was the name given to Mrs O'Brien. She had the largest number of children in the village. She wasn't an attractive woman. Neither was her husband an attractive man. But tonight Mrs O'Brien looked different. She wore make-up and her hair was freshly washed and combed.

'That's a change,' my uncle said.

'He'll have her pregnant again,' the teacher protested.

Other couples appeared on the street, husbands and wives who were never seen out together. Some were linking arms.

All the pairs walked ingratiatingly close to one another.

'What is this?' the teacher asked anxiously, 'what's happening?'

'Strange,' said the uncle.

Later when the pub closed we walked down the street together. On the doorway of the house next to ours a man and his wife were standing. She wore her Sundays and he leaned heavily on her shoulder.

'I know he's leaning on her,' said the uncle, 'but for him that's a lot.'

Two girls were sitting on the window ledge of the house at the other side.

'Come in for a cup of tea, Jack,' one said.

My uncle hesitated.

'Ah, come on, Jack,' said the other, 'it's early yet.'

The young teacher stood at the other side of the street, legs crossed, back propped against the wall. He looked gangly, wretched and lost.

'Care for a drop of tea?' the uncle called across.

Suddenly the teacher sprang into action. He checked first by looking up and down to confirm that it was really he who was being invited. Then fully assured he bounded across the roadway, a mad hunger for companionship in his eyes.

The uncle explained to the girls how he would have to see me safely indoors but promised he would be back in a matter of moments. He suggested that meanwhile they start the proceedings without him. Courteously, or rather gallantly, the teacher stood aside to allow the ladies first passage indoors. One giggled but covered her mouth in atonement when the other nudged her to stop. In our own house the uncle poured me a glass of milk and we sat at the table for a spell.

'See what I mean?' he said. 'I told you things would never be the same.'

I nodded that I fully understood.

'Was that why you shaved tonight?' I asked.

'No,' he answered, 'but I can see now it was a good job I did.'

13
A Tale of Two Furs

Jack Murphy was a sportsman. By this I mean that it was no trouble at all to him to disappear for a week should there be a succession of sporting events coinciding with a full wallet and a disposition to travel.

He owned a prosperous business and had an excellent wife who always tried to make allowances for him.

He also had a sister-in-law who was forever trying to come between the couple. Jack's was a childless marriage and after fifteen years of 'constant endeavour', as he was fond of putting it, there still seemed to be no likelihood of an addition to the family.

The sister-in-law had come to live with them not long after her husband died. Unkind people intimated that she nagged him to death while others held that he drank himself to death to be free of her.

To give him his due Jack Murphy tolerated her. He never let her feel that she might be an outsider and even his worst enemies were prepared to compliment him on that score. He listened to what she had to say with attentiveness. He would nod politely now and again as she rattled on but he never once indicated by word or gesture whether he agreed with her or not.

Jack's wife Kitty was always expansive in her gratitude to her husband. She was well aware that nobody else would endure Margaretta for so long. She told him so frequently and Jack, because he loved his wife, would always say; 'ah 'tis a thing of nothing Kitty girl. Where else would she go but to her own?'

From the day he quit his teens and inherited the family business Jack always owned a greyhound or two. Like most greyhound owners he was always patiently waiting for that exceptionally good one to turn up. Sometimes he bred a middling dog or bitch but none had come near equalling any local track records not to mind breaking one. He persevered. He brought good pups and he mated his brood bitches with the best dogs money could buy. For years he had mixed luck. The most promising pups never lived up to expectations but he was in some way compensated when an average dog ran above himself and won the occasional race.

Then when he least expected it he found himself, one season, with a truly talented bitch. She ran unbeaten in her first five starts and qualified, with little difficulty, for the final of an important sweepstake in Ballybunion.

He trained her for the event as he would any other of his charges and she responded by reaching the height of her form at the proper time. At this stage in her career she was well known. Sportswriters in the national dailies and evening papers predicted a bright future. Like the true doggy man he was Jack Murphy kept his mind to himself. He had high hopes but it would never do to divulge these. The prospect of a big let-down in the long term was always on the cards. As the day of the sweepstake final drew near he was tempted to consult local handlers but on the advice of his veterinary he decided to trust to the bitch's natural talents.

On the morning of the big event Jack took his car to the garage and had it greased and cleaned. As he drove back to his home friends and neighbours stood in their doorways and wished him good luck for the night. He acknowledged each and every salute. Somehow he felt that a new responsibility had been thrust upon him. He was possessed of the natural fatalism of all greyhound fanciers but now for the first time he realised that his fellow townsfolk had entrusted him with the onerous task of improving the town's image. Many would be making the journey later that evening to cheer the bitch to victory but Jack was the captain so to speak. He was the very spearhead of the assault.

At home in the kitchen he kissed his wife goodbye. She held him longer than was normal for her. She knew that this was one of the most important occasions in his life. Finally she released him and from the folds of her purse withdrew a small bottle. It was partly filled with blessed water which a thought-ful neighbour had brought back from Lourdes. She allowed a few drops to spill over her fingertips. This she applied to his forehead making the sign of the cross as she did so. She sprinkled the remainder of the water on the bitch. At this stage Margaretta entered the kitchen. Jack knew she would be in-capable of wishing him good luck. It was not in her make-up.

'I'll be back some time tonight,' he told his wife, 'or, if not, I'll be here early tomorrow.'

'We all know the words of that song,' the sister-in-law an-nounced to nobody in particular.

'Now, now,' said Kitty, 'that will do you. 'Twould be more in your line to wish him luck.'

'Luck is the grace of God,' Margaretta retorted sharply. Jack refused to be drawn into the argument.

'You can get Timmy Kelliher to walk the other dogs,' he told his wife. 'Tell him I'll fix up with him tomorrow night.'

Saying not another word he led the dog from the kitchen.

He had already removed the cushions from the back seat of the car and covered the floor with a good depth of fresh straw.

'You and me,' he confided to the wide-awake hound, 'will show the lot of 'em a thing or two tonight.' Then he drove off, not heeding now the God-speeds and the waving hands. He was gone but seconds from the kitchen when the sisters had it hot and heavy between them.

'God knows when we'll see him again,' Margaretta spouted, 'it could be days and it could be weeks and then again he might take it into his napper to come back no more. I wouldn't put it past him now that he has the broad road between him and his home.'

'He said he'd be back tonight,' Kitty replied testily, 'and back he'll be.'

'So you say,' said Margaretta, 'but I expect the likes of that when I see it before me.'

'It's none of your business anyway,' Kitty cut her short. 'He's the boss of this house and I don't know where you get the right to criticise him.'

'Oh you needn't tell me who's the boss here,' Margaretta shouted back. 'I know my place. I've been put there often enough.'

The argument wore itself out after a while but nothing was settled. There was always the danger that it would flare up again.

Ballybunion track was crowded for the feature event of the night, the sweepstake final. The bitch was quoted liberally enough but her price shortened as Jack's friends and neighbours began to arrive. Eventually she was installed a firm favourite at five to four. Jack had been fortunate to get her at fours as soon as the prices went on the boards. He had on twenty-five pounds which meant that he stood to win a hundred pounds in addition to the two hundred and fifty pounds stake money should the bitch cross the line first.

As before all big events there was a sudden silence when the field of six were placed in their respective boxes. The tension mounted as the hare whistled up to the traps and when the dogs broke there was a mighty cheer, each of six contingents shouting for its fancy. The bitch broke well and was second as they came round the first bend.

At the second bend she was third and at the third she was in exactly the same place. Now the roars of the crowd were intensified and women could be heard screaming as the dogs entered the straight. It was here the bitch showed her real talent. She saw an opening next to the rails, took it like a flash and with it the lead for the first time. She won comfortably.

From all sides Jack was pummelled and patted by well-wishers. Supporters fought with each other to shake his hand. Jack said little. The one phrase he kept repeating to nobody in particular was 'What did I tell you? What did I tell you?'

He kept saying this over and over until his admirers departed to draw their money from the bookies.

An hour after the race Jack was entrenched in the corner of a public house lounge with a large number of friends seated protectively around him. At his feet sat the bitch. Under his seat was the trophy, a solid silver cup with the figures of six greyhounds inscribed around its middle. In his wallet was the money he had collected from the bookmaker. Also there was the cheque for two hundred and fifty pounds from the sweepstake. The cup had been filled and refilled with brandy and champagne.

Jack Murphy felt good. He had never felt so good before.

In his hand was a glass of whiskey. He dipped his fingers in the glass and rubbed them against the bitch's mouth. Her reaction was to lift her head and look around wide-eyed at the strange faces. All were loud in praise of her performance.

'What did I tell you?' Jack Murphy said. 'What did I tell you?'

A tall figure entered the lounge and a hush fell. People nodded respectfully and drifted aside as he moved towards Jack and the sitting hound.

This was Mister McKechnick the English buyer. He was as well known on Irish dog tracks as he was on English ones. He was known to be a decent man and consequently he was admired and respected wherever he went. He had a good name as a buyer. It was said of him that he never looked for bargains. He always paid what a dog was worth, no more and no less.

He beckoned to the barman.

'Fill a drink for the house,' he said quietly. When his bidding was done all present drank his health. Then Jack Murphy rose from his seat. He was a trifle unsteady but he was far from being drunk.

'Fill them up again,' he said to the barman.

'You have a class bitch there sir,' McKechnick complimented him.

'Thank you sir,' Jack returned. The two men chatted amiably while those within earshot respectfully withdrew. Business was business and nobody wished to stand in the way of a fair deal.

'What would you say she's worth?' McKechnick asked out of the blue.

'You're too sudden for me,' Jack answered. 'I would have to think that one over for a while.'

'Put some sort of estimate on her,' McKechnick urged.

Jack pursed his lips and scratched his head. He looked at the bitch and he looked at McKechnick. He looked at the floor and he looked at the ceiling. He looked at the serious, expectant faces ranged around the lounge and yet he was reluctant to fix a price. He realised that McKechnick was not a dawdler. Rather was he a busy man with little time on his hands.

'I would say sir,' said Jack in his most earnest fashion, 'that she's worth every penny of twelve hundred quid.'

'What you say to nine hundred?' the Englishman asked with a smile.

'I would say eleven hundred,' Jack responded with another smile.

'It looks rather like a thousand then, don't it?' McKechnick said with a hearty laugh.

'It do indeed,' Jack answered with another laugh.

McKechnick extended his hand and Jack took it in his. There was a handclap from the crowd.

'I'll give you my cheque,' McKechnick whispered, 'when things quieten down a little.'

Jack nodded agreement. McKechnick beckoned to a small, moustached man at the door.

'My man will take charge of her now,' he said.

As the bitch was being led away Jack suddenly bent down and impulsively flung his arms round her.

'Goodbye my little darling,' he said with tears in his eyes. 'Goodbye and good luck to you.'

At McKechnick's suggestion Jack accompanied him to his hotel. In the residents' lounge the Englishman handed over the cheque. Jack took a ten pound note from his wallet and thrust it into McKechnick's pocket by way of a luck penny. After that they had several drinks.

'You'll be my guest for the night of course,' McKechnick suggested. Jack had no objection. At twelve the Englishman announced that he was about to retire.

'I'm going to Limerick Races tomorrow,' he explained, 'and I don't want a hangover for the day.'

'I'm bound for those very same races,' Jack revealed, 'so I think I'll hit the sack too.'

In Limerick they fared well. During the two days of the races they backed several winners. McKechnick had good connections and the information he received proved most valuable. At night they would do the round of the city's pubs, joining in sing-songs and making new friends. On the final night there were several in the party. They had a hectic time between dancing and singing. Bottle after bottle of champagne was drank. At midnight McKechnick announced that he proposed to withdraw on the grounds that he intended travelling to the Curragh Races on the morrow. He asked Jack if he would care to accompany him. On the spur of the moment Jack agreed.

Quite a large party left Limerick for the Curragh the following morning. Jack rode with McKechnick, a titled lady who owned several racehorses, a bookmaker and two unattached, middle-aged ladies, friends of the titled lady.

Their good luck held at the Curragh. They had a golden rule about daytime drinking. Under no circumstances was anybody to touch a drop until five-thirty in the afternoon. McKechnick had a theory that betting and drinking did not go hand in hand. They had bets on four races. They won on three.

McKechnick declared more than once that Jack had brought them good luck. At five-thirty they repaired to the Grandstand bar where they proceeded to drink gins and tonics. After an hour the party was a merry one.

At six-thirty the titled lady got on the phone to a Dublin theatre and booked seats for the night's performance of a play which, she told Jack, had been favourably reviewed in all the dailies of the previous Tuesday. Jack slept soundly throughout the performance. He was loud in his praise after the final curtain had come down.

He remembered little after that. The night passed in a haze. During a meal in one of the city's more celebrated hotels he fell fast asleep. When he woke up he found himself in strange surroundings. He was in a comfortable bed in a bright, fully carpeted room. There was a chambermaid, dressed all in white, shaking his shoulder.

'They said I was to call you not later than half-past eleven sir,' the chambermaid informed him.

'Who said?' Jack asked.

'Your friends sir. It's Sunday and last Mass is at twelve. I've brought you some tea. I'll leave it here.'

She carefully placed the tray of tea things on a chair near the bed. Then she left the room quietly. Painfully Jack raised his head from the pillows. More painfully still he eased himself from the bed. He dressed slowly as though his body was covered with sores and needed to be treated with the utmost gentleness. He found his way downstairs and thence to the church.

Mass went by like a dream. It gave him all he could do to rouse himself at its conclusion. He struggled back to the hotel, went directly upstairs and straight to bed. The next time he woke he felt refreshed. He located his clothes and went through the pockets. His money was intact. He lay back on the bed glad that it had not been stolen.

Then for the first time in days he remembered his wife and as soon as he thought of her he thought of Margaretta. He could sense her gloating in the background. Thinking about his wife filled him with remorse. He could see the hurt in her eyes as the sister lorded it over her. There came a knock upon the bedroom door, gentle yet firm.

'Come in,' Jack called. It was the chambermaid who had awakened him the morning before. Again she carried a tray.

'What day have we?' Jack asked.

'It's Monday sir.'

'Great God almighty!' Jack exclaimed, 'and will you tell me what time is it?'

'It's eight o'clock in the morning sir.'

Upon hearing this he groaned and buried his face in his hands. He ran his fingers through his hair and groaned again and again.

'Is something up sir?' the chambermaid's voice was filled with alarm.

'I wish I was dead,' said Jack Murphy.

For the first time he noticed the girl. She was young, no more than eighteen but she had a sympathetic face and sympathy was exactly what Jack needed just then. The source did not worry him. While she poured his tea he launched into a full account of his adventures. She listened carefully and when he had finished she nodded her head sagely.

'I wouldn't worry too much,' she told him. 'You still have the money and that's a good start.'

'Oh sure,' he said with an edge of sarcasm, 'but 'tis me and not you that has to face the music.'

'All you have to do,' she told him bluntly, 'is buy a fur coat for your wife. I promise you there won't be a word out of her

148

if you land back with a good quality fur coat.'

'A fur coat,' he said and pondered her suggestion.

'But where would I get one?'

'Look,' she said kindly, 'I have an hour off at twelve. If you like I could meet you outside and show you where to go.'

'Good God,' said Jack gratefully, 'that would be great, great entirely.'

At twelve o'clock she was as good as her word. At ten past they were walking up Grafton Street. At half past they had narrowed the selection down to two.

One was a musquash at one hundred and fifty pounds and the other a Canadian squirrel at hundred and forty. They decided upon the musquash.

'Listen,' said the salesman confidently. He spoke as if he were doing them a very considerable personal favour.

'Why not take both. You pay for them now. When you arrive home let her decide for herself. You can return the one she doesn't want and we will only be happy to refund your money.'

This seemed to be an excellent idea.

'There is one other thing,' said Jack Murphy to the salesman, 'my wife is a very thrifty sort of woman so like a good man will you knock down the prices a bit.'

'We shall have no problem at all in that respect,' the salesman assured them. He produced two price tags, one marked thirty and the other twenty-five pounds. He attached the thirty pound tag to the musquash and the twenty-five to the Canadian squirrel. Jack returned with his parcels to the hotel where he bade goodbye to his young friend. He thrust a ten pound note into her hand as they parted.

It was late that night when he arrived home. It goes without saying that he was coolly received. His wife had no word of welcome for him, no word that is, until he produced the parcels. Proudly he ripped them open. He presented her with the musquash explaining that the other was on appro.

His wife was enchanted. She pressed the coat against her body and caressed it with her free hand.

That night Jack Murphy slept the sleep of the just. In the morning he received his breakfast in bed. His wife sat on the edge fondly watching him as he ate.

'I have good news for you,' she said.

'What would that be?' Jacked asked absently.

'You needn't bother to return the other coat. Margaretta thinks it a steal at twenty-five pounds and she's decided to keep it.'

14
THE HANGING

There is no sight so grotesque or pathetic as the dangling frame of a hanged man. It is also an affront to human symmetry. There is no parody so wretched and when Billy Fitz and John Murphy first saw Denny Bruder's body hanging from the crossbeam in Looney's shed they were bemused for some moments by the almost comic presentation of slack hands and slanted head. From the church nearby, as if by arrangement, came the muted tolling of the Angelus bell.

Billy moved first. He touched the hanging foot nearest him and when nothing happened he pushed it gingerly with his palm. The body unexpectedly started to gyrate slowly. The screams of the boys were simultaneous. They ran terrified from the shed.

Denny Bruder had first come to the village about five years before. He was a motor mechanic by trade. He took a lease of Looney's shed and in a short while built a reputation as an efficient man who knew all there was to be known about motor cars. You could not call him morose. Glum would be a more fitting word. He was gentle with children and he never resented their curiosity. He was not the best of mixers and mostly he was to be seen alone going for walks or visiting the cinema where pictures were shown every other night.

In the beginning he was never known to enter a public house and he showed little interest in the local girls but this could have been because they showed little interest in him. He was not the handsomest of men. He was medium-sized with a rather bulbous nose and thick lips. However, he was far from being repulsive. His was a dour sort of face. Older women in the village described it as homely. In time people came to accept him as part of the local scene.

Shortly after Denny Bruder's arrival Imogen Furey invested in a second-hand car. Imogen was the wife of Jack Furey the cattle-jobber. Jack already had a car but, as Imogen told anybody who might be prepared to listen, he was away from home so often at cattle fairs all over the country that they might as well not have a car at all. While Jack was away Imogen would visit his fields outside the village to count the cattle and to see if any wandering animals had broken down fences or forced entry. She would do this in all kinds of weather and since the fields were the best part of a mile from the village she was often in receipt of a discomfiting drenching and this, in addition to the time wasted, was one of the chief reasons why she felt the need of the car. There were two children, both girls, but these were away at boarding school for most of the year.

The car was an old model and if it burned more than its quota of oil it suited Imogen's needs nicely. When it broke down one evening as she was returning from counting the cattle she sent for Denny Bruder who towed it to his shed. It transpired that the fan belt was broken. There was nothing else the matter. While Denny was installing a new belt Imogen suggested that he give the car a complete overhaul. She left it in his care and late the following afternoon he delivered it to her door. She was surprised at the reasonableness of his fee.

Thereafter they became good friends and he took a personal interest in the behaviour of the car.

Midway through his second year Denny Bruder invested

in some up-to-date garage equipment. This improved his business considerably and in his third year he found himself with more money than he actually needed. He looked about for a safe spot to invest it.

It was Imogen Furey who solved his problem. Envious neighbours were fond of saying that she knew everything about everybody. By this they inferred that she knew more than was good for her. Uncharitably they would hint that if she paid more time to her own business and less to the business of others she would be better off. This, of course, was not the case at all. Imogen Furey was an eminently successful woman by any standards. Her husband was reputed to be the wealthiest man in the village. Her home had every conceivable amenity. She dressed well and was a leading figure on local committees. Her children were boarded at one of the most exclusive schools in the country. On the surface, at any rate, hers was the sort of thoroughly satisfying existence which was bound to provoke resentment and jealousy.

When Denny Bruder confided to her that he had money to spare she asked for time to consider his situation. It was her experience that house property or land were the safest means of ensuring a profitable return from investment. On the outskirts of the village was a two-storeyed house in relatively good condition. It had been on the market for some years but because its owner was asking too exorbitant a price it went unsold. She informed Denny that she was convinced the house could be bought for the sum originally asked. After an interval of three years she explained that the price was not in the least exorbitant by prevailing values.

Denny bought the house, handed notice to his landlady and moved in. For months he was rarely seen in public. After work he would spend most of his time indoors redecorating the rooms and generally restoring the woodwork, ceilings and anything else he found in disrepair. When he had finished indoors he started on the outside. It was early spring when he started on the neglected garden which faced the roadway. He planted shrubs and trees and showed an excellent sense of taste in his selections.

He painted the house front and windows with delicately contrasting shades. By late spring the job was completed. He was more than satisfied with his handi-work. He decided to sit back and await developments. All through the summer he confidently expected a proposal or suggestion of marriage through some medium from whatever candidates were available. The house was his chief bait. It was much admired by the villagers as was the garden. He worked hard and which was more important he was seen to work hard. He bought new clothes and invested in a small comfortable car. The months of summer wore on and when the trees began to shed the first autumn leaves he found himself still with an empty house. He was puzzled. He knew he was no lady-killer but he was also aware that there were many happily married men in the village far uglier and less well-off.

He started to visit the public houses. He never drank more than a glass or two of beer. He became friendly with some of the barmaids but that was as far as it went. He went to dances in the village hall and sometimes to neighbouring towns when the bigger, betterknown bands included these in their itineraries. He never danced. He often tried but the girls he fancied were snapped up before he could get off his mark. Consequently he spent most of his time standing with other male onlookers at the rear of the hall.

That winter was one of the most miserable he ever spent. He missed the company of the other lodgers in his old digs. The house was unbearably lonely. To crown his misfortune he was smitten by a heavy dose of influenza. He was three days in his bed before anybody showed sufficient interest in his whereabouts to pay a visit to the house. His friend Imogen Furey eventually called. He thrust a muffled head from one of the uppermost windows and told her hoarsely that he was ill. At her bidding he dropped the key to the door at her feet. She was back in less than half an hour with a jug of chicken broth. She called again and again until he was fit to resume work.

At Christmas, to repay her kindness, he bought her a present of the most expensive perfume available. The Fureys, to give them their due, knew a decent man when they met one. At Jack's bidding, Imogen invited Denny to a meal one of the nights during Christmas. Afterwards they sat in front of the sitting-room fire drinking a special punch compounded by Imogen. The heat of the fire and the whiskey to which he was unused had the effect of totally loosening Denny's tongue. In a short while he had unfolded his tale of woe, confessing his loneliness and explaining his most pressing need.

The Fureys were moved first to concern and then to pity. At a late hour that night Jack Furey drove Denny home. In bed later on he asked his wife if there was anything she could do.

'He's a likely fellow,' Jack said, 'and by the cut of him I don't think he'd blackguard a girl.'

'He's no Romeo,' Imogen pointed out.

'Romeo's don't always make the best husbands,' Jack countered. Before she slept she promised she would look into it.

'I'll have to think of who's available,' she said thoughtfully. Jack Furey knew his wife.

'You'll come up with something,' he announced sleepily.

Through the spring Denny planted more shrubs and blooms. At his garage he worked hard. He had, by now, acquired more than a local reputation and motorists from neighbouring towns would patronise him occasionally. He took to dealing in second-hand cars and was soon making more than he ever dreamed possible. He bought a better car and went about more. On Saint Patrick's night he was invited to a party at Fureys. There were other people present. One of these was a girl from the nearby hill country. Her name was Nora Odell. She was auburn-haired and although exceedingly pale of feature was nevertheless quite an attractive girl in her late twenties. She was an indrawn, reserved sort. There had been talk that she had been seriously let down once by a neighbouring farmer but this was discounted as immaterial since almost everybody is subject to some sort of let-down at one time or another, the only difference being that there is never much revelation of these reverses by those who are at the receiving end.

Towards midnight all present gathered round the piano in the Furey sitting-room. Denny Bruder surprised everybody by proving himself to be the proprietor of a very fine baritone voice. The evening was a success. At Imogen Furey's suggestion Denny asked Nora Odell if he might call and take her out some time. She agreed and they settled upon a date. Unfortunately, it was a blustery, rainy night. For want of something better to do Denny asked her if she would like to see the interior of his house. At first she was reluctant but he seemed so genuinely put out that she relented.

After a tour of the bedrooms he asked her if she would like

to hear some records. He injected life into the sitting-room fire and chose a selection of Strauss waltzes. The evening was a happy one. She often came to the house after that.

Once he invited her to dinner. He prepared it himself. The main course consisted of curried chicken with the faintest echo of garlic for which she did not exactly care. Otherwise it was a first class meal. Denny explained that during his school holidays he used to help his mother in the kitchen of the hotel where she worked during the summer. He was an excellent cook and she would seize eagerly upon his invitations to dine in the house. Knowing her dislike of garlic he never used it when she was joining him for a meal. As the months went by Denny Bruder began to fall inextricably in love with Nora Odell. He never told her so. He was content to bide his time and wait for a suitable opportunity. Summer came and on Sundays they would motor to the seaside. Sometimes he would take her father and mother. He was now a constant caller at the Odell home. The senior Odells like him and Nora's brothers respected him. He was one of the best mechanics for miles and a chap never knew when he might be obliged to visit him.

One fine Sunday in August the pair sat on the grass at the end of a peaceful headland overlooking the sea. Beneath them the incoming tide was noiseless and the flat unbroken surface of the sea like a sheet of silver. Overhead the sun shone from a blue sky. Suddenly Denny Bruder placed an arm around Nora Odell's shoulder.

'I'd love if you married me,' he said.

'Would you?' she asked turning and looking at him directly.

'You know very well I would,' he told her.

'Kiss me,' Nora said. He kissed her awkwardly. After the kiss she took his hand and led him to the shore where the small waves broke listlessly at their feet.

'I'll have to tell my parents,' she said, 'and you will have to speak to my father, ask for my hand if you know what I mean.'

'That will be no bother,' Denny assured her.

'I'm sure he'll be pleased,' she said, as if she had known all along that their marriage was inevitable.

Denny Bruder was elated. Without taking off his shoes he ran in the water up to his knees and shouted to the heavens. 'I'm going to be married,' he called out. 'I'm going to be married to Nora Odell.'

They became engaged a fortnight later and a date was set for the wedding. Neither approved of long engagements and so it was that they decided upon the first Saturday of October. In early September, however, they were to be separated for a longish period. Nora's sister Bridie who was married in Wolverhampton was due to have her third child about this time. She wrote to Nora asking her to come and housekeep for her husband and two children.

Denny drove her to Rosslare which was the port most convenient. As he kissed her goodbye he suddenly realised how utterly empty his future would be without her. She had given his life a new meaning. He was, in fact, a different person since meeting her. People had told him so. It was expected she would be gone for a fortnight. This would allow her a week to prepare for the wedding upon her return home.

During her absence Denny spent every second night visiting the cinema. He always occupied the same seat in the balcony. One night a woman called Angela Fell, the wife of a local shopkeeper, happened to be seated next to him. Midway through the film she suddenly said, 'Oh, oh.' She said it loudly so that her voice carried to the corners of the balcony. Then she left her seat and occupied another at the end of the last row. After the show there was much conjecture. Several different reasons were put forward to justify the uncharacteristic behaviour of Angela Fell. Those who sat nearest to Denny Bruder spoke from a position of authority. A young man who sat directly behind Mrs Fell said that Denny was seen to suddenly lift his hand when she uttered the exclamation already described. As to the exact location of the hand prior to its being lifted, he was heard to say, 'where the hell do you think it was?'

By implication this meant that Denny Bruder's hand was placed on an area of Angela Fell's anatomy which might best be described as out of bounds. There were some who flatly refused to believe this. There were others who refused to believe otherwise. Nobody thought of asking Angela Fell. Of all the women in the village she was the least communicative and the sharpest-tongued.

After this incident Denny Bruder was a marked man. People in his vicinity on the balcony would be paying more attention to him than to the screen. Denny had no idea he was under observation. A week passed and a teenage girl from the nearby countryside arrived late at the cinema. She fumbled her way to a vacant seat next to Denny Bruder. Couples nudged each other in anticipation. Nothing happened till near the end of the film. Then she left her seat and went outside. There was no longer any doubt in the minds of the villagers.

Some were filled with pity, others with indignation. Imogen Furey found herself in a dilemma. It was she who introduced Nora Odell to Denny. Clearly she would have to do something. One night in bed she asked Jack if he was asleep. He had been away for several days buying calves in the western counties and had earlier retired to bed. Jack Furey was awake. Painfully Imogen related the details of what had transpired in the cinema.

'What am I to do?' she asked.

'Leave well alone,' Jack Furey advised her, 'marriage will knock all that sort of thing out of him.'

'I feel responsible,' Imogen persisted.

Jack lay silent. He could feel sympathy for Denny Bruder. He remembered what it was to be lonely, to be so sick with desire that little was beyond contemplation. Essentially he was a tolerant man who was prepared to go out of his way to make allowances.

'I once caught a girl by the knee in the cinema,' he said trying to make light of the matter.

'But you knew her,' Imogen replied.

'I thought I knew her,' Jack Furey said, 'she was no damned good.'

Imogen knuckled him playfully on the side of the face. 'It's no laughing matter,' she said seriously, 'I wish to God it was.'

They spoke far into the night. At Jack's suggestion she agreed to do or say nothing until Nora came home. Shortly before her return Nora received two anonymous letters. The day before her actual departure she received a telegram from her older brother which stated coldly that he would be meeting her at Rosslare. She had been prepared to discount the two letters until she read the telegram.

It had been agreed that Denny Bruder would meet her. If her family saw fit to change the arrangement there must be something afoot. Both brothers were waiting when she disembarked. There and then they made her pen a letter to Denny acquainting him of a change of mind on her part. At first she refused point blank but when they threatened to deal with Denny themselves she reluctantly agreed. She would have liked to hear his side of the story. Family was family however and in the end where else was a person to fall back. She succeeded in convincing herself that she was doing the correct thing. In the days that followed Denny Bruder called repeatedly at the Odell farmhouse. He refused to stop calling even when the older brother appeared at the front door one evening with a shotgun in his hands. In the end both brothers dealt him a severe beating.

After this he concealed himself for a time. It was when word of the beating reached the Furey household that Imogen decided to act. Jack had left early that morning. Before his departure he asked Imogen to pay a visit to Nora Odell.

'If either of them two brothers so much as looks at you sideways I won't like it and you can tell 'em so.'

Imogen nodded. As soon as Jack had gone she made out a shopping list. Shortly before noon she betook herself to Fell's grocery. Mick Fell carefully scrutinised her order which was a substantial one.

'I'd like a word with Angela while you're getting those ready,' Imogen said.

'Of course,' Mick Fell agreed. 'Go straight through.'

Imogen followed a narrow passageway into a tiny kitchen. It was a suffocating place with a gleaming hot Stanley range dominating the entire scene from one corner. Angela was bent over a small table chopping meat.

'I hope I haven't come at a bad time,' Imogen said.

Without a word Angela strode past her towards the shop.

Imogen could hear her voice plainly. 'I thought I told you I didn't want to see anybody while I was working. What sort of god-damned nit are you anyway?'

'Look at the size of the order she's given me,' Mick Fell replied defensively.

'I don't care if she gave you herself,' Angela screamed at him. 'I don't want people collaring me in that hellhole.'

'What do you want of me?' she asked with hands on hips when she returned.

'Simply this,' Imogen answered tonelessly, 'what did Denny Bruder do to you at the cinema?'

'You have a blasted neck you have,' Angela hit out.

'His hopes of marriage are wrecked,' Imogen forestalled her. 'Tell me what really happened. I promise you no one else will ever know.'

'Get out of here,' Angela advanced a step. Imogen refused to give ground.

'I'm not leaving this kitchen till you tell me,' she declared. 'A man's whole future depends on what you say to me this morning. I'm asking you as one mother to another if Denny Bruder molested you in any way that night at the pictures. If he is innocent you have a duty to perform. If not say so and I'll walk out of here this instant.'

'I have nothing to say to you,' Angela returned. 'Please leave now.'

Imogen took a step in the direction of the shop but turned finally and faced Angela squarely.

'If this gets into court,' she said, 'and it well may, you won't get off so lightly.'

The veneer of hard independence faded from Angela's face. 'Court,' she echoed stupidly.

'Yes, court,' Imogen pressed her advantage. 'That's where they take people who destroy a person's character.'

'I've destroyed nobody's character. I never put a hard word on the man.'

'That may be but you never put a good word on him either.'

They stood facing each other. From the shop came the voices of other customers. There was laughter when Mick Fell passed a wry remark. Angela crossed to the table where she resumed her chopping. She spoke over her shoulder. 'He did nothing to me,' she said. 'I left my seat because there was a smell of garlic. When he belched I found it overpowering so I went to another seat.'

'You might have said so before this,' Imogen said accusingly. In the shop she collected her groceries. She resolved to go to Odells that afternoon. First she would see Denny Bruder. Not for the first time she marvelled at the unnatural reticence of women like Angela Fell. Involuntarily she shuddered when she thought of the evil begat by the silence of such people.

As she crossed the roadway to her home the Angelus rang. She blessed herself as did others who were on the streets. Between the peals she could hear the distant cries of children.

15
THE CURRICULUM VITAE

Fred Spellacy would always remember the Christmas he spent as a pariah, not for the gloom and isolation it brought him nor for the abuse. He would remember it as a period of unprecedented decision-making which had improved his lot in the long term.

Fred Spellacy believed in Christmas. Man and boy it had fulfilled him and for this he was truly grateful. Of late his Christmases had been less happy but he would persevere with his belief, safe in the knowledge that Christmas would never really let him down.

'Auxiliary Postman Required'. The advertisement, not so prominently displayed on the window of the sub post office, captured Dolly Hallon's attention. Postmen are nice, Dolly thought and they're kind and, more importantly, everybody respects them. In her mind's eye she saw her father with his postbag slung behind him, his postman's cap tilted rakishly at the side of his head, a smile on his face as he saluted all and sundry on his way down the street.

If ever a postmaster, sub or otherwise, belied his imperious title that man was Fred Spellacy. It could be fairly said that he was the very essence of deferentiality. He was also an abuse-absorber. When things went wrong his superiors made him into a scapegoat, his customers rounded on him, his wife upbraided him, his in-laws chided him. His assistant Miss Finnerty clocked reproachfully as though she were a hen whose egg-laying had been precipitately disrupted. She reserved all her clocking for Fred. She never clocked at Fred's wife but then nobody did.

'Yes child!' Fred Spellacy asked gently.

'It's the postman's job sir.'

Fred Spellacy nodded, noted the pale, ingenuous face, the threadbare clothes.

'What age are you?' he asked gently.

'Eleven,' came the reply, 'but it's not for me. It's for my father.'

'Oh!' said Fred Spellacy.

Dolly Hallon thought she detected a smile. Just in case she forced one in return.

'What's his name, age and address child?'

'His name is Tom Hallon,' Dolly Hallon replied. 'His age is thirty-seven and his address is Hog Lane.'

Fred Spellacy scribbled the information onto a jotter which hung by a cord from the counter. He knew Tom Hallon well enough. Not a ne'er do-well by any means, used to work in the mill before it closed. He recalled having heard somewhere that the Hallons were honest. Honest! Some people had no choice but to be honest while others didn't have the opportunity to be dishonest.

'Can he read and write?'

'Oh yes,' Dolly assured him. 'He reads the paper every day when Mister Draper next door is done with it. He can write too! He writes to his sister in America.'

'And Irish? Has he Irish?'

'Oh yes,' came the assured response from the eleven year old. 'He reads my school books. He has nothing else to do!'

'Well Miss Hallon here's what you must get your father to

165

do. Get him to apply for the job and enclose a reference from someone in authority such as the parish priest or one of the teachers. I don't suppose he has a *Curriculum Vitae?'*

'What's that?' Dolly Hallon asked, her aspirations unexpectedly imperilled.

'The jobs he's had, his qualifications ...'

Fred Spellacy paused as he endeavoured to find words which might simplify the vacant position's requirements.

'Just get him to put down the things he's good at and don't delay. The position must be filled by noon tomorrow. Christmas is on top of us and the letters are mounting up.'

Dolly Hallon nodded her understanding and hurried homewards.

Fred Spellacy was weary. It was a weariness imposed, not by the demands of his job but by the demands of his wife and by the countless recommendations made to him on behalf of the applicants for the vacant position. Fred's was a childless family but there was never a dull moment with Fred's wife Alannah always on the offensive and Fred the opposite.

Earlier that day he had unwittingly made a promise to one of the two local TDs that he would do all within his power for the fellow's nominee. Moments later the phone rang. It was the other TD. Fred had no choice but to make the same promise.

'Don't forget who put you there in the first place!' the latter had reminded him.

Worse was to follow. The reverend mother from the local convent had called, earnestly beseeching him not to forget her nominee, a genuine vessel of immaculacy who was, she assured him, the most devout Catholic in the parish. Hot on her heels came others of influence, shopkeepers, teachers and even a member of the civic guards, all pressed into service by desperate job-seekers who would resort to anything to secure the position. Even the pub next door, which had always been a *sanctum sanctorum*, was out of bounds. The proprietor, none more convivial or more generous, had poured him a double dollop of Power's Gold Label before entreating him to remember one of his regulars, a man of impeccable character, unparalleled integrity, unbelievable scholarship and, to crown all, one of the lads as well!

'Come in here!' There was no mistaking the irritation in his wife's voice. She pointed to a chair in the tiny kitchen.

'Sit down there boy!' She turned her back on him while she lit a cigarette. Contemptuously she exhaled, revelling in the dragonish jets issuing from both nostrils.

Fred sat with bent head, a submissive figure. He dared not even cross his legs. He did not dare to tell her that there were customers waiting, that the queue at the counter was lengthening. He knew that a single word could result in a blistering barrage.

'Melody O'Dea,' she opened, 'is one of my dearest friends.'

Her tone suggested that the meek man who sat facing her would grievously mutilate the woman in question given the slightest opportunity.

Again she drew upon the cigarette. A spasm of coughing followed. She looked at Fred as though he had brought it about.

'Her char's husband Mick hasn't worked for three years.'

Alannah Spellacy proceeded in a tone unused to interference, 'so you'll see to it that he gets the job!'

She rose, cigarette in mouth, and drew her coat about her.

'I'll go down now,' she announced triumphantly, 'and tell

Melody the good news!'

When Tom Hallon reported for work at the sub post office at noon on the following day Alannah Spellacy was so overcome with shock that she was unable to register a single protest. When Tom Hallon donned the postman's cap, at least a size too large, she disintegrated altogether and had to be helped upstairs, still speechless, by her husband and Miss Finnerty. There she would remain throughout the Christmas, her voice fully restored and to be heard reverberating all over the house until she surprisingly changed her tune shortly after Christmas when it occurred to her that the meek were no longer meek and must needs be cossetted.

Alannah Spellacy had come to the conclusion that she had pushed her husband as far as he would be pushed. Others would come to the same realisation in due course. Late in his days, but not too late, Fred Spellacy the puppet would be replaced by a resolute, more independent Fred.

Fred Spellacy had agonised all through the previous night over the appointment. In the beginning he had formed the opinion that it would be in his best interest to appoint the applicant with the most powerful patron but unknown to him the seeds of revolt had been stirring in his subconscious for years. Dolly Hallon had merely been the catalyst.

Fred had grown weary of being told what to do and what not to do. The crisis had been reached shortly after Dolly had walked out the door of the post office.

That night, as he pondered the merits of the score or so applicants, he eventually settled on a short list of four. These were the nominees of the two TDs, his wife's nominee and the rank outsider, Tom Hallon, of Hog Lane.

He had once read that the ancient Persians never made a

major judgment without a second trial. They judged first when they were drunk and they judged secondly when they were sober. As he left the post office Fred Spellacy had already made up his mind. He by-passed his local and opted instead for the privacy of a secluded snug in a quiet pub which had seen better days. After his third whiskey and chaser of bottled stout he was assumed into that piquant if temporary state which only immoderate consumption of alcohol can induce.

From his inside pocket he withdrew Tom Hallon's *Curriculum Vitae* and read it for the second time. Written on a lined page neatly extracted from a school exercise book it was clearly the work of his daughter Dolly. The spelling was correct but the accomplishments were few. He had worked in the mill but nowhere else. He had lost his job through no fault of his own. Thus far it could have been the story of any unemployed man within a radius of three miles but then the similarities ended for it was revealed that Tom Hallon had successfully played the role of Santa Claus for as long as Dolly Hallon could remember. While the gifts he delivered were home-made and lacking in craftsmanship his arrival had brought happiness unbounded to the Hallon family and to the several other poverty-stricken families in Hog Lane.

'Surely,' Fred Spellacy addressed himself in the privacy of the snug, 'if this man can play the role of Santa Claus then so can I. If he can bear gifts I can bear gifts.'

He rose and buttoned his coat. He pulled up his socks and finished his stout before proceeding unsteadily but resolutely towards the abode of Dolly Hallon in Hog Lane.

He had been prepared, although not fully, for the repercussions. The unsuccessful applicants, their families, friends and handlers, all made their dissatisfaction clear in the run-up to Christmas. They had cast doubts upon his integrity and ancestry in language so malevolent and scurrilous that he was beyond blushing by the time all had their say.

One man had to be physically restrained and the wife of another had spat into his face. He might not have endured the sustained barrage at all but for one redeeming incident. It wanted but three days for Christmas. A long queue had formed at the post office counter, many of its participants hostile, the remainder impatient.

From upstairs came the woebegone cronawning of his obstructive spouse and when the cronawning ceased there came, down the stairs, shower after shower of the most bitter recriminations, sharper and more piercing than driving hail. He was very nearly at the end of his tether.

'Yes!' he asked of the beaming face which now stood at the head of the ever-lengthening queue. There was no request for stamps nor was there a parcel to be posted. Dolly Hallon just stood there, her pale face transformed by the most angelic and pleasing of smiles. She uttered not a single word but her gratitude beamed from her radiant countenance.

Fred Spellacy felt as though he had been included in the communion of saints. His cares vanished. His heart soared. Then, impassively, she winked at him. Fred Spellacy produced a handkerchief and loudly blew his nose.

16
THE REEK

The bog was a mixture of browns and greys, grey where the sun had bleached the exposed turf banks and the misshapen reeks of yesteryear which stood along the margin of the roadway. In the moonlight the grey turned to silver but the brown remained sombre even when stars danced and the heavens seemed on fire. When the weather was fine the bog was my playground. Every goat-path, bog-hole and goose-nest was as familiar to me as the lanes and streets of the nearby town where I lived. I knew the titles of the turf banks and the names of the reek owners. I knew the sod depth of every bank and the quagmires where asses and ponies sank to their haunches. This was because I spent most of the summer days with two ancient relatives who lived in a tiny thatched house on the edge of the bog. They were brothers. Their names were Mr Chamberlain and Sir Stafford Cripps. These, of course, were not their real names. Rather were they sobriquets invented by the locals on account of the resemblance the pair bore to the British politicians Neville Chamberlain and Stafford Cripps. The Second World War was well under way when I discovered the bog and there was an abundance of Rommells, Montys and McArthurs so christened because of forecasts they might have made regarding the outcome of the war or because of certain characteristics relating to the famous generals.

Mr Chamberlain was the older of the two brothers. He was lean as a whippet, bald as a coot and reticent to the point of muteness. Sir Stafford on the other hand was as talkative as he was outgoing. Both were on the old age pension. It was Sir Stafford who tackled the ass and went to town on Fridays to cash the pension vouchers. Mr Chamberlain would not demean himself with such mundane matters and only went to town on Sundays to attend Mass. The pair got on famously. Sometimes there were disagreements but these were short-lived. I remember one such. It was early September. The turf was harvested and new reeks were beginning to appear daily on the roadway. The brothers had earlier cut, stooked and re-stooked two sleans of turf and this stood now in donkey stool-ins in the bog on the heather-covered turf bank which had supplied them with turf for generations. It would have to be transported from the bank to the roadway where it would be built into a reek.

Mid-August to mid-September was the recognised time for drawing out. The passages to the turf banks were dry and firm but later they might be rendered impassable by heavy rains. When this happened the turf remained in the bog until the late spring of the following year and the owners had to make do with the remains of old reeks and occasional sacks laboriously drawn on their backs from the stranded stoolins.

'It's time,' Mr Chamberlain announced as we sat on the low wall which fronted the house.

'And I say it's not time,' Sir Stafford countered.

'And why so do you say that?' Mr Chamberlain asked, 'when I say otherwise.'

'I say that,' said Sir Stafford, 'because the man on Hanafin's wireless made a forecast of rain.'

'And what do he know?' Mr Chamberlain asked derisively, 'that couldn't tell one end of this bog from the other no more nor the ass.'

'He knows plenty,' Sir Stafford persisted.

'There will be no rain tomorrow,' Mr Chamberlain spoke with finality. 'The wind is from the right point and there's heating in it and if there's heating in it then by all the laws the sun will be along after the wind.'

To give confirmation to his belief he raised his head and turned his thin, sensitive nose into the wind. I did likewise. The sea was less than five miles distant as the crow flies and sometimes there was a tang of salt in the air. Other times, especially after high tides, there would be a strong fragrance of sea wrack. Often there was the unmistakable odour of decay but it was always possible for a man of experience and judgement to smell out any rain that might be likely to move inland in the course of time.

'There's no rain in that, no rain at all.' So saying Mr Chamberlain rose unsteadily from his seat and sauntered down the roadway towards the passage which led to the turf bank. He had aged more during this summer than he had in all the years since I knew him. He still walked erectly if somewhat irresolutely. There were hints of debilitation in all his steps.

'There's a stagger to him,' Stafford Cripps whispered. I knew what this meant. A stagger was taken to mean that a man was nearing his end, maybe not immediately nor for a considerable time. It was a telling factor, however, from which there was no reprieve.

Later that evening I was invited to participate in the drawing out. I was to be in charge of transport. Cripps was to be posted on the turf bank where he would assist in filling the ass rails. Mr Chamberlain was designated reek maker. He had somewhat of a reputation in this field and it would have been unthinkable to have invested him with a less onerous task.

173

The following day broke bright and clear. There was little or no wind but the air was crisp and cool. The sky was free of cloud and it looked as if the day would be a fine one. Mr Chamberlain had been correct in his forecast for as the morning wore on and the sun climbed higher in the sky it grew distinctly warmer. Each time I heeled the ass cart and emptied a fresh load Mr Chamberlain nodded his appreciation but made no attempt to start building the reek. He merely indicated where he wanted the cart heeled. He knew exactly what he was doing of course. Earlier he had counted the donkey stool-ins and made an estimate of the space he would need to contain the entire harvest. He measured his ground with even paces and then with boot lengths for exactitude until a rectangular base was plotted. I had seen him make reeks before. There was no more meticulous builder in the bog. This time he seemed to be more fastidious than ever. He weighed the turf sods with greater care and occasionally he placed a particularly large and well-shaped brick to one side. These would be used later in the clamping.

All morning we worked and as we did the September sun ascended the cloudless heavens. For every step it took upwards the reek took another. At noon we broke for food. This had been painstakingly prepared by the brothers. Mr Chamberlain had lighted a fire during one of my journeys to the turf bank. Atop it sat a kettle of boiling water, a continuous jet of steam shooting from its shapely spout. Wrapped in white muslin was a sizeable wedge of boiled bacon and in another cloth was a pound or so of fresh cheese. There was also a loaf of home-made bread and a solid slab of butter. As soon as the tea was drawn we set about eating. In between mouthfuls Sir Stafford would make a pronouncement.

'There is no sauce like bog air.'

I was too preoccupied to comment one way or the other.

'Plain food is the best food,' from Sir Stafford again. It went on like this until we had eaten and drank our fill. Then we sat back and relaxed awhile. This was the best part of the day. Other men who were occupied as we were came to join us in order to debate the course of the war. Mingled scents of heather and woodbine imposed themselves fleetingly over the pedestrian odours of the roadway. There was time to savour the sunlit beauty of the bogland while the men spoke on and on of important happenings. Endlessly larks rose carolling from hidden haunts in the heather. The air was clear as far as the eye could see. The little haze there was had long since been burned up by the hot sun. The talk now dwelt on the subject of townspeople.

'I have seen them,' Sir Stafford was saying, 'and they racking their hair before stooking the turf. I have seen them and they wearing low shoes only fit for dancing and they trying to operate a slean.'

Here Mr Chamberlain made one of his very rare contributions to the proceedings.

'I seen the first of the turf-cutting townies at the start of the war,' he said. 'They came in droves when the coal got scarce. I seen strange things but I never before seen the likes of these men. They had bread with meat in the middle of it. You could only see the edge of the meat. The rest was covered by bread above and below. There is no way you could inveigle me to eat meat I couldn't see.'

'It must be sandwiches you're talking about,' Sir Stafford put in.

'The very thing. The very thing indeed. That was the name

given to them.'

The talk wore on. It was of times gone by when men worked for coppers and promises and often turned over in their beds at night in an effort to dispel the hollow growling of hunger in empty stomachs. They spoke of spailpíns and labourers who worked from dawn till dark and who had nothing at all to show for their labours in the end, nothing but stooped backs and strained limbs. They spoke of the immeasurable value of book-learning as the one true avenue of escape from drudgery and expressed regrets for the way they had neglected their books in favour of youthful dalliance.

'A schoolmaster now,' someone said, 'he earns a sovereign a day and he don't bend his back.'

'No wonder they're cracked,' Sir Stafford commented, 'money like that would go to any man's head.'

Elsewhere the fate of the world was being decided. Far away in Cairo, Churchill and Roosevelt were meeting with Chiang Kai Shek and in southern Italy fierce battles were raging as the Allies endeavoured to advance north-wards. We sat drowsily in the lee of the reek grateful for the warm sunshine. The conversation started to flag with the realisation that the time had come to resume work. Later there would be another break for what was known as 'the evening tay'. This consisted of a panny of tea and a slice or two of bread and butter. It was generally a hurried affair at which no time was wasted. There was still some talk but the conversation had lost much of its sparkle. I was despatched in search of the donkey. He had not ventured far. There was an abundance of good grass and wild clover at hand on the margins of the roadway. He allowed himself to be recaptured without resistance as though he knew instinctively that the day was far from being down and there was no point in prolonging his legal recess. I tackled him to the cart without difficulty and in a short while we were working as a unit once more. The pace had quickened as if by agreement although not a word passed between us. There was an urgency to the work now. The pressure would have to be maintained if we were to finish by evening. After 'the evening tay' the old men seemed to grow tired. So did I but it would never do to give the impression that one was unable to pull one's weight. The pace was relentless now but no quarter was asked or given. It would not be too long before the last of the stoolins was on the roadway. It was heartening to see the decrease in their number.

The reek was really taking shape now, assuming that peculiar symmetry with which only a countryman could invest it. There was something here above and beyond blueprints and drawing boards. There was an instinctive insight into the secret shape of the land itself and into this was fitted unobstructively the dark contours of the reek. Instead of standing out it fitted in like a patch into a quilt. I noticed too that it did not run in a precise parallel line with the roadway. Its strongest shoulder better buttressed than the others stood in the face of the prevailing south-westerly wind. Immense knowledge about the peculiar tantrums and exact route of this wind was essential if the reek was to survive the vicissitudes of winter and any reek, no matter how large, was, after all, only as strong as its weakest point. From time to time Mr Chamberlain would walk slowly round its base searching for inadequacies. Often too he would remove himself from the immediate vicinity of the reek and survey it with a critical eye from a distance. He observed it from every angle and from every posture. One moment he would be standing on the tips of his toes and the next he would be lying prone. He inspected it from his haunches and he went so far as to kneel in the centre of the roadway to determine if the upward inclination was gradual enough. Nothing was left to chance. Never before had he been so finical. As the evening wore on he grew somewhat irritable but this passed when the reek reached a certain stage in its development.

Sod by sod, foot by foot it rose to its smoothly tapering roof until the last ass-load had been deposited on the roadway. All that was left on the turf bank was a carpet of dust and tiny cadhrawns. Sir Stafford and I untackled the ass. At once he rolled over and over on the dusty roadway, braying ecstatically. When he had rolled his fill he flicked his hind legs defiantly and cantered down a narrow causeway where a green patch of good grass advertised itself. The reek was finished except for a few final touches. The clamping was impeccable. Hardly the width of a grass blade divided sod from sod. Sir Stafford now took a turn around it, pausing to inspect a particularly impressive piece of cornering. With the aid of the ass-cart Mr Chamberlain mounted the reek and sat astride its roof. I stood by with a gabhail of assorted sods. Occasionally there would be a surgical extension of his hand and I would tender a sod. He might or might not accept it, favouring another of different size or shape. It seemed to me that he was overdoing it. Now with hindsight I know that he was merely a thorough and conscientious craftsman who selected sods and parts of sods the way a poet might select words or phrases essential to the immaculate completion of the work in hand.

Also the finished work would be submitted for critical analysis although it would be true to say that the most just and impartial critics of all would be the north-easterly and south-westerly winds. These were the lads who wouldn't be long pinpointing flaws. The accredited critics came that very evening. These were accomplished reekers themselves. All the reviews were favourable with the exception of the usual carper or two whose own reeks could never stand up to penetrating criticism.

'That won't be knocked aisy,' one white-haired on-looker essayed.

'That,' said Sir Stafford Cripps pointedly, 'won't be knocked at all.'

The days passed. Autumn went its way in a flurry of russets and winter appeared, unexpected as always but predictably harsh and cold with mighty storms that ranted and raged cross the countryside. The reek was not found wanting under the onslaught. It was its maker who was to prove suspect. In January he contracted a heavy cold and because he would accept advice from nobody and stay indoors like a sensible fellow he developed pneumonia and had to be removed to hospital. His condition weakened and one spring morning when the last of the wild geese were winging their way northward he died in his sleep. Shortly after Mr Chamberlain's demise Sir Stafford was smitten by influenza but the neighbours, fearful lest he should be swept away like his brother, maintained a constant vigil and by the middle of March he was on his feet once more, hale and hearty. The reek stood for the remainder of that year without interference. Sir Stafford made do with old turf which lay in a shed at the rear of the cottage. When the season for turf-cutting was under way he hired three young men from the locality to cut a brace of sleans. The reek he left untouched. His decision was not questioned. Artistically it was the best designed and most shapely fabrication of its kind to have been constructed on the roadway for generations. During its third year there was considerable shrinkage but such was the character of the design in the original structure that there was still no unevenness nor was there the slightest evidence of depression from end to end. Now denuded of its original brown by the years of wind and rain, its bleached exterior gave the impression that it had been frosted all over. On clear nights, under an unshrouded moon, it seemed as if it were a great rampart of silver.

Then of a gusty March evening a large band of travelling people appeared at the entrance to the bog. They liked what they saw. They were impressed by the green of the cutaway and if it was a faded green itself the ponies, horses and asses of which the train was mainly comprised were anything but choosy. Down the road they came in three multicoloured, horse-drawn caravans, flanked and trailed by a motley assortment of the most heterogeneous mongrels imaginable. It was a swift-moving but silent caravan. Its occupants, animal and human, were feeling their way. The faces of the menfolk who led the caravan horses were blue with cold. Their noses ran freely. From time to time they would press a finger against one side and expel the rheumy contents of the free nostril with snorts and grunts. As they approached the reek a flock of children suddenly appeared from the interior of the caravans and started to play games on the roadway, contriving, at the same time, to stay in front of the three caravans. When all had passed it was plain to be seen that the reek would never be the same again. There were gaping black holes and cavities along the side nearest to the roadway. Sir Stafford had never taken his eyes from the passing train. Still he had been caught napping by the children's diversions. He knew from long experience that a search of the caravans would reveal nothing. The stolen turf would be instantly and secretively jettisoned at the first sign of danger. Sir Stafford was furious. The reek was now scarred and ulcerous and prey to rain and storm. It would collapse completely in a matter of weeks particularly since it was now certain that further inroads would be made into its already gutted side.

Night came. The fires of the travellers burned brightly in the deep of the bog. Sir Stafford sensed that they would stay awhile, in all probability till the end of April. The reek would stand no chance.

He had looked upon it as a monument to the late Mr Chamberlain. He foresaw a time when it would have naturally and gracefully disintegrated just like its maker but he had never allowed for the intolerable rape of that afternoon. He knew exactly what must be done. In the cottage hearth he built a great fire of heavy black sods. When the coals glowed red he transferred them to a tin bucket and made straight for the reek. The wind was from the east but it was dry and crisp. He selected a favourable spot and withdrew several sods from the base. These he replaced with the glowing coals. For the freshening breeze it was a labour of love to achieve the rest.

17
DEATH BE NOT PROUD

The land meant everything to Mick Henderson. The cardinal rule of his long life was its preservation. Envious neighbours whose own land had become run down through neglect and laziness would have outsiders believe that he loved the land more than he loved his wife and certainly more than he loved his family. This was not so. He had been fond of his wife when he married. He had remained fond of her through storm and calm over the years and even now when the physical aspect of his marriage was becoming something of a memory he treasured her companionship in a way that only long attachment can foster.

He would have been hard put to explain his obsession with the land. His wife understood fully and there were others like himself in the valley who felt as he did. These would be silent, tight-lipped men, not without humour and not given to vindicating or modifying what would seem to be an extraordinary pre-occupation with the soil.

At seventy Mick Henderson found himself in a quandary. Labour was becoming impossible to come by. Factories were shooting up like thistles in the nearby towns and cities. Whatever workforce was available in the area was almost completely absorbed. Even his regular workman had deserted him for lucrative shift work and a five-day week. The latter was something of a joke amongst the farming community. All the holdings supported herds of milch cows and during the heavy milking periods these needed constant attention.

Once when endeavouring to hire a workman Mick was asked if he would settle for a five-day week. 'You can have a one-day week in the winter,' Mick had told him, 'but until such time as we have a five-day cow there will be no five-day week.'

He had gone so far as to offer free Sundays during the peak periods and occasional days off for special events but there was no competing with the attractions of the factories. He cut down his herd to a manageable size although he was still heavily in debt from having put three sons and two daughters through boarding schools and colleges. There was another son, Mikey, named after himself, a black sheep of sorts, who disappeared one morning when he was barely sixteen after a vicious row regarding his attitude towards further schooling. That was nearly ten years before. Mick Henderson knew his son's address in England, knew he was doing well as a charge-hand in a Coventry factory, knew enough in fact to make Mikey feel downright uncomfortable if he ever suspected such paternal interest.

The others had no feeling for the land, no concern about it. On his seventieth birthday he had betaken himself to the city to consult with his eldest son, Maurice, who was a solicitor there. After listening carefully for over half an hour Maurice submitted his opinion.

'Your safest and your easiest course,' he said dispassionately, 'is to sell out and live here in Dublin or if city life has no appeal for you there is nothing to prevent you from buying a comfortable house in the country. The money you would make from the sale would clear your debts and leave you with more than sufficient to ensure a comfortable life for mother and yourself until the end of your days.'

His second son, Eddie, was a dentist. Married with two

children, he operated from a small surgery attached to his home in the suburbs. Late as it was when Tom called he found Eddie up to his eyes in work. Very late that night they sat round the sitting-room fire and talked about the land. It was impossible not to like Eddie and his wife but they had little to offer by way of a solution. They also felt that selling the land would be the best way out.

It was the third son, Martin, a civil servant, who supplied the obvious answer. Mick had a job finding his house in the sprawling, estate-cluttered northside of the metropolis. Snugly seated in the back seat of a taxi he passed row after row of newly-erected, two-storeyed houses. After numerous en-quiries they eventually discovered the estate. Another search and they located the house. It stood amid hundreds of others which looked exactly alike.

'How in the name of God does anyone live here?' he had asked undiplomatically when Martin and his wife met him at the door.

'You get used to it,' Martin said enjoying his father's perplexity.

In spite of his first impression he was pleasantly surprised by the interior of the house. It had a heartening spaciousness in contrast to what he had expected.

'You have a fine home Martin,' he announced by way of conciliation.

'It's only a few hundred yards from the school,' Martin's wife said, 'and that's what really matters.'

After the usual preliminaries Mick settled down to the business of outlining his problems. Martin and his wife listen-ed sympathetically while he explained about the new factories and the scarcity of labour.

'The last thing I want to do is sell it,' he finished.

'The logical thing as far as I can see is to bring Mikey back from Coventry,' Martin suggested.

'Will he want to come back?' Mick asked.

'I have no doubt that he will,' Martin assured him.

Mick Henderson considered this for some time. It was a thought that had always been at the back of his head. All he needed was someone, other than himself, to suggest it. He was aware that Martin and Mikey were as close as brothers could be despite the distance that separated them. In age there was hardly a year between them. It was to be expected, therefore, that Martin would put forward a strong case for the youngest brother. Mick Henderson decided that he would find out how forceful Martin's advocacy might be.

'That's all very fine,' he said disinterestedly, 'but has he the feel for the land?'

'Why wouldn't he?' Martin hastened to reply, 'he's your son isn't he?'

'You're my son and you have no feel for it. Neither have Maurice or Eddie.'

'Look,' Martin pleaded, 'Mikey is different. He's only good with his hands. He was a hopeless scholar. If you had kept him at home when he kicked off the traces that first time he'd know it all now and you wouldn't be worrying about labour.'

''Tis easy be wise after the event,' Mick Henderson said. He suspected that Mikey might have the true feeling for the land but there was no way he could be certain. He resolved to probe further.

'What guarantee have I that he won't flog the farm as soon as I pass on?' he asked.

'That's a chance you'll have to take but let me tell you this. Mikey is hardly likely to flog it when it's going to be his livelihood. You know as well as I that he knew how to handle livestock. That time before he ran away he had no objection to working on the farm. What he objected to was school.'

'Agreed,' Mick Henderson returned, 'but there's many a young lad will volunteer for anything to escape school.'

'I happen to know,' Martin's tone was really serious now, 'that if he doesn't come home this year he won't come home at all.'

'Did he say this?'

'Yes.'

'Then I suppose I had better contact him. What if he says no?'

'That's one thing he won't say,' Martin assured him. After this conversation Mick Henderson had no doubt in his mind that Martin and Mikey had discussed his position in depth. On his way home by train he had ample time to think. His one fear was that the land might be sold after his death but this would happen anyway if Mikey refused to come home. He remembered when the farm had been signed over to him by his own father. It had been a bright May morning close on forty years before. He had no idea what his father's business in the neighbouring town might be when he instructed him to tackle the black mare to the family trap. By mid-day he was the legal owner of the land. He had in no way pressurised his father although he had dropped hints that he was thinking of getting married. It was somewhat different in his case. The true feeling for the land was there. His father knew this, knew that the green pastures to which he had devoted the best years of his life would be safe for another generation. It was so important that Mikey have this feeling for the acres which would shortly be under his care. Mick Henderson knew everything there was to be known about the land. Over the years he had discovered its idiosyncrasies and failings and learned painstakingly how to turn deficiencies into advantages. The land had its own unique characteristics, its own vague, imperceptible contours, its inexplicable portions of soft and hard, wet and dry, barren and lush.

On the surface the fields were like any other in the district but he knew better. His father had been a source of constant help as he endeavoured to discover the true lie of the land. Now that he knew all there was to be known it was high time the knowledge was passed on. He would announce his decision to his wife Julia as soon as he got home. She would be pleased. He was aware that she secretly pined after her youngest son although, like all mothers, she became somewhat resigned to his absence as time went by.

The proper thing for me to do, Mick thought, is to impress upon him without seeming to do so the value of well-treated land. I will show him that while human life is to be valued more than anything else, that which sustains it should be valued no less. I will pass over and my wife will pass over but the land will remain. We are only passing through, mere tenants at best. The land will be there forever to nurture my seed and the seed of my seed. Somehow he would try to get these feelings through to Mikey. If the genuine consciousness was there this would be no problem. If Mikey did not fully respond all would not be lost. At least he would not sell and the land would be saved. If one generation failed to throw up a man with love for the land the next generation was sure to compensate. Who could tell but he might live to see a grandson blessed with the appropriate and peculiar disposition so difficult to define.

Mikey Henderson arrived home during the second week of spring. The roadside hedgebanks were bright with clusters of early primroses and along the sides of the avenue leading to the old farmhouse were healthy clumps of daffodils and irises in various stages of flower. It was a good time to come home. During the first months he made many mistakes but Mick was not slow to notice that he never made the same mistake a second time. He was uncannily adept with all sorts of machinery. He understood cattle and most important of all he knew how to husband his strength. He fitted perfectly into the pattern of things.

Mick watched his progress with the keenest interest. Who knew but some evening he might see Mikey with his hands on his hips surveying the sheen of a freshly-ploughed tillage field or shading his eyes against a summer sun on the headland of a meadow ripe for cutting.

With the coming of summer the new green grass, luscious and fleecy, returned to the fields. The hedge-rows no longer bare hosted a thousand songbirds and the first of the long herbage took the naked look from the broad meadows.

The meadows would prove to be the chief of Mikey's problems that first summer. It wasn't a particularly good year for growth. The new crops were light and late and to crown the general misfortune of the farming community there was no labour available when the outlook was favourable for harvesting. The weather too was unkind. To say the least it was inconsistent. Fine days were few and far between and rarely succeeded each other. During this time came the worst calamity that could possibly befall. Julia Henderson took ill and had to be removed to hospital. All thoughts of harvesting had to be abandoned until she recovered.

It was two weeks before she was released. She had undergone a mild coronary. Her doctor warned that unless she cut down considerably in her everyday work there would be a recurrence. After her short stay in hospital she felt refreshed and the tiredness which had nagged her for so long seemed to have disappeared altogether. She herself declared that she felt twenty years younger and insisted in shouldering her full quota of chores. A young girl was found locally to help her. She agreed to stay until the schools reopened in September. Outwardly, at any rate, Julia Henderson seemed very much rejuvenated. She looked the picture of health and there was none of the breathlessness which she so often endured before her visit to hospital.

There was a general air of excitement all over the district when the weather changed for the better. Despite the fact that there was no immediate prospect of labour Mick and Mikey Henderson decided to make an all-out assault on the uncut meadows. All day they followed each other on two tractors. In their wake the tall grass fell in long parallel swathes. Julia and the girl brought their meals to the meadow. There was no tarrying for small-talk afterwards. As soon as they had eaten they mounted the cumbersome machines. The onslaught lasted until the first faint stars appeared in the late evening sky. The moment they finished they headed straight for the local pub. It wasn't that they especially needed a drink. It was the only place where they were likely to recruit labour. They were partly successful. It was first necessary to invest in several rounds of drink and to exhibit an interest in the welfare of likely prospects that was tantamount to fawning. This, with the offer of almost double the normal wage, was responsible for the extraction of three promises. Both Mick and Mikey were well aware that the trio in question were not exactly the cream of the crop. They would be late and they would put no great strain on themselves but they were labourers and if the weather held the produce of the combined meadows might be saved at the end of three days.

For most of the first day they turned and then tossed the freshly mown swathes. Late in the afternoon they made it up into windrows in preparation for the following day's cocking. This completed they broke off. That night the Hendersons listened avidly to the weather forecast. Prospects were still good. Mick and Mikey rose with the dawn. First the cows had to be milked. Then the milk had to be cooled and transported to the creamery. After that it was straight to the meadow. Everything else was secondary. The labourers arrived at ten o'clock and then the business of cocking commenced. First the crisp hay had to be gathered by the tractor-drawn, iron-toothed rake. Mikey attended to this particular function. He worked furiously supplying the needs of the cock-makers who worked in pairs. When the supply exceeded demand he would jump from the tractor and shoulder huge pikefuls of hay to the base of the developing cock. This was the hardest part of haymaking. One by one, slowly and painfully, the cocks went up until by the end of the second day half the entire crop was safe. The mid-day meal was brought to the meadow by Julia Henderson and the girl. On the third day Julia came alone. The girl had not showed up. Enquiry revealed that she had been at a dance the night before and was unable to get out of bed. Julia was not unprepared. She arrived at the meadow shortly after noon, just as the sky was undergoing a murky suffusion to the south-west. If rain was to come this would be the direction from which it would threaten. After the meal one of the labourers announced that he was unable to continue because of a stomach ailment. Mick guessed that the pace was not to his liking. The same man had shown himself to be somewhat of a shirker from the beginning. Mikey had heard him derogatorily remarking to one of his colleagues that if he was to die he wouldn't like it to be for a farmer.

Despite her husband's protestations Julia insisted in falling in by his side. They worked together, silently, at a corner of the meadow far removed from the other pair. Julia Henderson was the ideal farmer's wife. Always she had been by her husband's side when the need was there. Of solid farming stock herself, she was aware of her obligations although these had often ranged from milking the entire herd to deputising at weddings and funerals. This was the unwritten law when labour was not to be had.

Now and then Mick would glance anxiously to the west and south where the ominous turgescence of massing clouds was slowly enveloping the otherwise clear sky. By his own reckoning he estimated that there were three, maybe four good hours left. Given that much time all the hay would undoubtedly be saved. He redoubled his own efforts and then without warning of any kind Julia Henderson heaved a massive, choking sigh. Mick stood helpless and appalled while she attempted to restrain with clutching fingers the terrible upheaval in her chest. Then just as suddenly her hands fell listlessly to her sides and she fell backwards noiselessly in a crumpled heap. Urgently Mick Henderson bent and whispered an act of contrition into her ear. There was no disputing the fact that she was dead. He stretched her legs gently and folded her hands across her bosom.

Then he sat by her side awaiting the arrival of Mikey with the next rake of hay. The young man sensed something was wrong. He dismounted slowly from the tractor and read the news in his father's face. He knelt by his mother's side and kissed her on the lips and forehead. He smoothed back the hair from her face and lifted her head so that he could rest it on the pillow of hay. Then he rose and looked at the sky.

'Let's get on with it,' he said. At first Mick Henderson looked at him uncomprehendingly. Then the logic of it dawned on him.

'What about the two?' he asked, pointing to where the labourers were building a cock at the other end of the meadow.

'What they don't know won't trouble them,' said Mikey dismissing the question. Slowly his father rose. Already Mikey was adding to the half-made cock. Instinctively his father followed his example.

Before departing for another rake-up Mikey laid a hand on his father's shoulder.

'She would understand,' he said. 'I don't have to tell you that. When the job is done we'll take her indoors. Then I'll go for a priest.

So saying he mounted the machine and in a matter of seconds was again raking the ever-decreasing wind-rows. Mick Henderson cast a glance at his dead wife and then his eyes followed his youngest son. Beyond doubt here was a man with a sound sense of priorities, a man with a true feel for the land.